THUNDER ON THE TENNESSEE

The Texans closed to within a few hundred feet of the enemy when heavy firing broke out to the right. Men began dropping, but the charge didn't waver. Ahead Willie could see a Yank lieutenant getting his men into line to face the charge. Then Captain Reynolds gave the order to fire, and an accurate volley from the Texans staggered the Federal line and broke their resistance.

Willie and the others ran through the camp, shooting holes into enemy soldiers and taking close to a hundred prisoners. Out of breath from the hard charge up the hill, Willie fell to his knees and tried to catch his wind.

"It's not over yet, boys!" Lieutenant Bales shouted, pointing his sword at another Yank camp to their left. "Let's go get them!"

Willie couldn't believe his ears, but the lieutenant wasn't jesting. Just beyond the edge of the regimental camp they'd captured stood another. The rest of the brigade was already engaging it, but a Yank colonel was waving his sword in the air and rallying his command.

Just then the ground around them exploded with a volley of rifle fire, and three men fell to the ground mortally wounded.

MORE PAGE-TURNING ADVENTURES FROM PUFFIN!

Adrift Allan Baillie
Bones on Black Spruce Mountain David Budbill
Bristle Face Zachary Ball
The Call of the Wild Jack London
Canyon Winter Walt Morey
Dogsong Gary Paulsen
Drifting Snow James Houston
Hatchet Gary Paulsen
Jericho's Journey G. Clifton Wisler
Little Brother Allan Baillie
My Side of the Mountain Jean Craighead George
On the Far Side of the Mountain Jean Craighead George
The Raid G. Clifton Wisler
Red Cap G. Clifton Wisler
River Runners James Houston
Save Queen of Sheba Louise Moeri
Sentries Gary Paulsen
Toughboy and Sister Kirkpatrick Hill
Tracker Gary Paulsen
White Fang Jack London
Wilderness Peril Thomas J. Dygard
Winter Camp Kirkpatrick Hill
The Wolfling Sterling North
Woodsong Gary Paulsen

THUNDER ON THE TENNESSEE

G. CLIFTON WISLER

PUFFIN BOOKS

PUFFIN BOOKS
Published by the Penguin Group
Penguin Books USA Inc., 375 Hudson Street, New York, New York 10014, U.S.A.
Penguin Books Ltd, 27 Wrights Lane, London W8 5TZ, England
Penguin Books Australia Ltd, Ringwood, Victoria, Australia
Penguin Books Canada Ltd, 10 Alcorn Avenue, Toronto, Ontario, Canada M4V 3B2
Penguin Books (N.Z.) Ltd, 182-190 Wairau Road, Auckland 10, New Zealand

Penguin Books Ltd, Registered Offices: Harmondsworth, Middlesex, England

First published in the United States of America by Lodestar Books,
an affiliate of E.P. Dutton, 1983
Published in Puffin Books, 1995

7 9 10 8 6

THE LIBRARY OF CONGRESS HAS CATALOGED THE LODESTAR BOOKS EDITION AS FOLLOWS:
Wisler, G. Clifton.
Thunder on the Tennessee.
"Lodestar Books."
Summary: Following his father's example, sixteen-year-old Willie Delamer joins the
Second Texas Regiment and leaves his beloved Texas to fight for the Confederacy.
[1. United States—History—Civil War, 1861-1865—Fiction. 2. Texas—Fiction.]
I. Title.
PZ7.W78033Th 1983 [Fic] 82-21057 ISBN 0-525-67144-7

Puffin Books ISBN 0-14-037612-7

Printed in the United States of America

for my uncle, Earl C. Wisler,
who first took me to Shiloh

THUNDER ON THE TENNESSEE

Before Shiloh, jaunty songs like "Dixie" and "The Bonnie Blue Flag" filled the air. Proud regiments boasted of never yielding the field. Men laughed and talked of chasing the Yankees back across the Ohio, of being home for Christmas. It's been said the South never smiled after Shiloh.

THE NIGHT WAS BLACK, lifeless. It was like the inside of some long forgotten cave, damp and eerie, filled by a swirling mist that could make a man's flesh crawl. There were no stars that night. They'd been swallowed by the blackness, by the clouds that had brought buckets of April rain—rain that had waterlogged the roads, turned creeks into impassible rivers, changed fields into mucky swamps where a man could sink to his knees.

A terrible hush fell over the land. Aside from the occasional chirping of a cricket or the croaking of a frog, a silence had frozen the air. The birds had flown away. Perhaps they sensed the stillness, were forewarned of the events that would change trees and men and even the eternal river.

A small campfire burned along a narrow lane cut through the dense forests of oak and pine. All around it shadowy figures lay, their backs against trees, huddled in groups of four or five. It was like some army of the dead awaiting the order to spring to their feet and fall into line, to march across some nether region reserved for soldiers.

A single figure stirred, different somehow from the others. Slight of frame, more boy than man it seemed. But there were the eyes, the manner of a soldier. He was not uncommon for that army. And if he wasn't as stout as the others, the long black musket on his shoulder made him an equal.

The young man moved his hands across the small fire, feeling the warmth flow through him from the flames. What was left of the boots his father had bought in Houston only weeks before stood near the embers. It would have suited the soldier to bare his feet and dry the soggy stockings that had been glued to his toes those last two days. But the sergeant had warned him of taking guard duty lightly.

On the stock of the old musket were scratched two initials, W. D.—Willie, short for William, Delamer. His name, the same one his father had taken proudly to Mexico with General Taylor. It was the name etched on the tombstone of his grandfather, the one who'd died at Goliad with Colonel Fannin.

"Delamers always stand in the first line of battle," his father had said.

Even at fifteen, Willie had been stirred by the words. Now, half a year and a thousand miles later, he would come to understand the meaning of those words.

Rumors of fighting had flown through Corinth for a week. There were no rumors now, though. The campfires of the Yanks could be seen on the high ground a couple of miles distant. Sounds of boats on the river and the smell of coffee and ham were carried by the wind. And there was a shadow of death hanging over it all.

If only the stars were out, Willie thought to himself. If only the night weren't so black, so cold. He stared at his pitiful boots. Taking a small stick, Willie scraped mud from the heels. Already large holes were worn in the soles. Another day's march and he would have to wrap his feet in strips of cloth like the others.

It wasn't how he'd imagined the eve of battle. In Houston the whole outfit had been decked out in splendid uniforms. Now those uniforms were worn and in bad need of washing, just as the men underneath.

There was a sound behind him just then, and Willie cleared his head of all thoughts. He rose to his feet and swung the ancient musket in the direction of the disturbance.

"Halt!" Willie called out.

"It's only me," said a voice with the hard southwestern accent of the Brazos country.

"Password," Willie said nervously, drawing a bead on the voice.

"Comanche," the voice said.

"Advance and be recognized," Willie said, relaxing his aim.

"That you, Willie?" the voice asked, coming close enough to the fire to be recognized.

"You're not supposed to be movin' about," Willie told

the bearded private who'd been his neighbor John Hall only a few months earlier.

"Got kind of lonesome down there with all them boys from the coast, Willie," John said.

"You're supposed to stay with your sergeant," Willie said. "That's the colonel's orders."

"Heck, Willie, orders is orders, but if you was to ask me, there's too much drillin' and regulations 'round this place to suit me. We's the ones to put old Santa Anna on the run, remember? I been in a scrap or two, and I don't need no Frenchy-speakin' stick of a general givin' me a lot of fancy regulations."

"General Beauregard won at Fort Sumter and at Manassas," Willie said. "Besides, General Johnston's in command. He's a Texan, like you and me. Orders make sense. You can't fight fifty thousand Yanks like you would a Comanche war party."

"Fifty thousand Yanks," John said, laughing. "Why, I could stomp out half of 'em with a good turkey rifle. By tomorrow night them Yanks'll be scattered from Saint Louis to Baltimore."

"That's got nothin' to do with orders, John," Willie told the man. "You see them two stripes on my sleeve? Well, that means I'm in command this night. Now get back to your company."

"Command?" the man asked, laughing. "Heck, Willie, I knowed you 'fore you could keep your britches dry at night. Them stripes's pretty, but a man ought to remember his friends."

"Go back to your position, private," Willie said, swinging the musket around so that it bore on the other man's head.

"I'm goin'," John said, quickening his retreat. "Soldiers! Heck, he'll be a general hisself next week."

Willie turned back to the fire then. If only the stars were out, he thought to himself again. A night without stars was like a woman without a smile. There was something missing, something cold and dead as a tomb. Always before when things bothered him, he'd been able to look up into the sky and speak with the stars, feel himself welcome, at home—even if there were many miles between him and the simple wooden house above the Brazos that he knew as home.

Home. It was a word that warmed him. And if the stars had been there, those same stars that were shining over the cloudless skies of Texas, he might have felt something more. Here it was April, springtime. Willie'd never known such a chill to be in the air of Texas. Likely it was that godforsaken swamp of a Tennessee river bottom. Fighting Yanks in the mud!

Willie'd been gone half a year now. No, it was eight months. Back in September no one had known there was a war. Willie'd been down on the bank of the Brazos River with Travis Cobb. The two of them were dipping mesquite poles into the river.

It was like any other autumn afternoon, two friends enjoying a break from the blazing Texas sun. Whenever the heat and dust choked a man, the river was always there to restore life. The Brazos. The early settlers had named it the Arms of God. Truly it was. Everything good came from that river.

The trees and plants drew their life from it. The water for corn and vegetables was diverted from the creeks and streams that fed the river. Stock grazed beside its banks, and boys grew strong from the fish that could be plucked from its depths. Across the river, you could hear the eerie sound of the wind whistling through the canyon. Indians had once lived along those cliffs, and there was an ancient village and a sacred burial ground there.

"I've got one!" Travis yelled, shattering the smooth, almost mirrorlike surface of the river. "Ellie will have something to bake now," Travis said, hauling out a large catfish.

"If you clean it," Willie said, looking over the fish. "She hates to bone catfish."

"You help me, and I'll bet I can get you an invite to join us," Travis said.

"I can get an invite any time I want one," Willie said, smiling. "Your mama said so."

"That's because Ellie's got her eye on you, Willie. And she's a bad one about gettin' what she wants."

"She's too skinny for my taste," Willie said, turning back to the river to hide the blush that filled his face.

"You're skinny your own self, Willie Delamer," Travis said. "And you've got an eye for her, yes sir. I've seen the way you look at that girl. Just fourteen she is, and the winsome way will go with the years. Look to Ma. She's the prettiest woman in the valley."

"Don't you go writin' my name in any family Bible just yet, Trav," Willie said. The two of them laughed, and the lines went back into the river.

The fishing was interrupted by the noise of someone splashing through the river upstream.

"Early for the mail, Willie," Travis said. "And there ain't been a stage through here in months."

Willie took his old Mexican War musket and handed Travis his fishing pole. Several steps led the way to the road, and Willie waited there for the rider.

"Hold up there," Willie called to a young man on horseback, the dust of a hard day's ride covering his clothes. "You got business here?"

"If this be Big Bill Delamer's place," the rider said.

"And who are you?" Willie asked, leveling the musket so that the stranger filled its sights.

"Messenger from the state capital," the rider said. "I've got a dispatch for Mr. Delamer."

Willie stared hard at the man. The stranger was wearing some kind of gray uniform, and a cavalry saber hung at his side. But there was nothing dangerous about the man's face.

"I got to be ridin' to the house myself," Willie said, setting aside the musket and walking to his horse. "I'll take you there."

Willie had a sixth sense about things, and something warned him this messenger was no casual passerby. His suspicions were justified. Willie's father acted strangely after reading the dispatch, and the courier did not even bother to stay to supper.

"Who was the man?" Willie asked his father after dinner. "The one with the gray shirt. He seemed to ride with a purpose."

"He brought a letter from the government in Austin," Willie's father told him.

"From Governor Houston?" Willie's younger brother James asked.

"No, from a new government," Willie's father told them all. "Sam Houston's been dismissed from office."

"What?" Willie's mother asked. "Not Sam Houston?"

"He made a speech for the Union," the man explained. "Sam spoke out some against breaking away."

"Then the talk's true," Mrs. Delamer said. "We've joined the Montgomery Confederacy."

"With others," Willie's father said. "Most of the South's in it now, excepting Maryland and Kentucky. Missouri seems split on the issue."

"There's to be trouble then, isn't there, Papa?" Willie asked.

"Likely to be a war," the man said. "We're raising an army. There's already been trouble in Virginia and South Carolina."

"Those hotheads in South Carolina are always stirring things up," Mrs. Delamer said, gesturing to Willie's married sister Mary to help clear the table. "Can't go and fight a war over Calhoun and those old sword-rattlers."

"They've given the western army to Sidney Johnston," Willie's father said. "And they've offered me a regiment."

"Really, Papa?" Willie asked. "A whole regiment? That means you're a colonel!"

"I forbid it," Willie's mother said. "You fought the Mexicans. They can find somebody else."

"Who?" Willie's father asked. "Henry King, I suppose. Maybe some other poor fellow already lame from a Mexican cannon fragment will step forward. It's a duty, Elizabeth."

"Duty," Mrs. Delamer grumbled, taking the plates to the kitchen. "You men and your passion for duty'll get you all killed."

A hush fell over the room, and Willie glanced around. Mary and her husband, Tom, were silent. Little Jamie, only nine, played with his dinner fork. Willie's brother Sam, nineteen, whispered to his wife, Helen. Behind them in a crib Sam's two baby sons gurgled quietly.

"I forbid it," Mrs. Delamer said again, clearing away Willie's plate. "I simply won't have it, you hear."

But all of them knew the decision would be up to Bill Delamer, not his wife.

That night when most everyone was asleep, Willie listened to his father pacing on the wooden porch of the house. The boy slipped off the end of the bed quictly so as not to disturb Jamie. Slipping a pair of trousers over his nightshirt, Willie then walked through the house and met his father on the porch.

"Awful late for you to be about, son," his father said.

"Heard you pacin', Papa," Willie said.

"Bad enough that I've got to be doing it," the man said. "Doesn't make it any better to have company."

"I know," Willie said. "But I couldn't help myself. I got so many questions runnin' around inside my head. Papa, I don't understand about all this talk of the Union splittin' up or we bein' another country and such. Now there's talk of a war, too. What's it all about?"

"Well, Willie, Mr. Lincoln moved the Federal army into Virginia. He says he's trying to preserve the Union, that it's not legal to break away from the old country. The South formed a new nation, the Confederate States. Now I guess we'll have a war to decide if we stay independent or become part of the United States again."

"Seems kind of stupid to me," Willie said. "Wasn't so long ago they wouldn't let us be part of the United States."

Willie's father laughed, then spoke again.

"Son, I know what you're thinking. Ten years we fought to convince the Congress to let us in. Then we fought the Mexicans to stay in. Now we're going to fight our own people to get back out."

"Doesn't make much sense," Willie said.

"Most wars don't make a lot of sense," the man said, sitting down on a wooden bench beside the door and waving Willie over beside him.

"There's got to be a reason to it, Papa," Willie said. "I could understand fightin' the Comanches like you did, fightin' for your home or your family. I'd fight the Mexicans to be free of their laws like you and Grandpa did. But how come we're goin' to fight our own people?"

"Well, the Yanks call it a war against the slaves," Willie's father told him.

"Slaves?" Willie said. "What've they got against slaves?"

"Nothing," the man said, "against slavery."

"Papa, how come we're fightin' a war for slavery? I've never even seen a slave. They say they're dark as night. I've never seen anybody darker than a Mexican, and he wasn't a slave."

"Downriver, near Waco, there are lots of them. They work the cotton fields."

"I never been to Waco, Papa," Willie said. "I never seen a cotton field. You think we ought to fight so these people down to Waco can keep their slaves?"

"I never asked a man to work for nothing, Willie," the man said, putting a rough old hand on his son's shoulder. "My grandpapa left France because there was no freedom there. My own papa died at Goliad so we could be free. No, son, I won't go to war for those Waco slaveholders."

"But you're going just the same. Why?"

"You see, Willie, what's really at stake is the deciding. If something's to be done about slaves, then the people to decide are Texans and Virginians and Georgians. When somebody decides for you or sends an army down to make up your mind, you've got to fight it. If you don't, you're little better than a slave yourself. There's only one reason a man ever fights, and that's to protect his home and family, to preserve his way of life."

Willie glanced up at the sky a minute, then turned back to his father.

"It's why you fought Yellow Shirt and the Comanches all those years, isn't it?" Willie finally asked.

"And why he fought me," Willie's father said. "Because all a man ever has to know is where he belongs, where his home is. And if he doesn't fight to hold it, then he doesn't deserve to keep it."

Willie nodded, but his eyes were still full of confusion.

"Son, come on inside with me now. There's something I want to show you."

Willie followed his father inside. They stood together as his father took down a huge sword from the fireplace. It was polished and bright, a great sword worn by an ancestor, the Chevalier de Lyon, Willie's great-grandfather. The man had brought it to America. On the hilt was an inscription that told how the sword was a gift of the king of France.

"Do you remember the story I told you about this sword, Willie?" his father asked.

"Yes, sir," Willie said. "Great-grandpapa refused to take it down when they had the revolution in Paris. He brought it to New Orleans, changed his name, and we became Americans."

"He came here because he wouldn't back down from a fight. My papa died in the same way, Willie. Delamers always stand in the first line of battle. A lot of them have been killed that way, but we never ask another man to do our fighting, and we never turn away from responsibility.

"I'd hoped to have many years of riding at your side, showing you how to build the ranch and make yourself into a man. You understand most of what's important, though. When it comes time to stand on your own feet, you'll do it just fine. You know enough about animals to run this place now, and you're strong enough to build without destroying the old as you do it."

"Yes, Papa," Willie said.

"Now, you'd best find some sleep. I've got a busy day for you tomorrow. There's more than enough to do. Loading wagons, raising a company of soldiers, tending to the ranch."

"Good night, Papa," Willie said, feeling his father's tired hand on his shoulder once again.

"Good night, son," the man said.

2

NEWS THAT BILL DELAMER had been appointed to command a regiment of Texas volunteers spread rapidly along the Brazos. More than a few crusty old veterans of the Mexican War took out their muskets and prepared to follow the man who'd led them to victory in Mexico, and before that against the menacing Comanche bands of Yellow Shirt.

There was excitement everywhere. Every boy above the age of three was talking of joining up to chase the Yanks back beyond the Ohio River, out of Maryland, away from their sister states of the South so that men could tend to their own affairs.

Willie noticed, though, that his father had less of the enthusiasm of others. Once as they rode together along the eastern boundary of the huge Delamer ranch, Willie's father called to him to stop.

"Would you look at this land, son," the man said. "Land free as the wind and hard as rock. What manner of fool would die for a place as desolate as this?"

"It's home, Papa," Willie said. "I'd die for it."

"They say this earth isn't much good for growing things, Willie," his father told him. "They say nothing but cactus and mesquite survives here. But I tell you, it takes a strong man to grow up here, a hard kind of a man. This country's good for growing hard men, good women, honest folk. I'd not trade it for ten thousand acres of bottomland on the Mississippi."

"I wouldn't know what to do with farmland. I was born out here. It's all I know. Cattle and horses, life on the open range. It's all I need," Willie said. "Or want."

It was what he'd said to his mother when she'd announced he was going East for three years of formal schooling. Unable to argue her out of it, Willie'd ridden off to join his friend Red Wolf and hunt buffalo with the Comanches.

When Willie finally returned home, things had changed. The softness had disappeared, and it was a tanned and hard Willie who'd faced his father. Things had been different between them ever since. Willie noticed a faraway look in his father's eyes, and the man sighed.

"I brought you out to share this with you, Willie," his father said. "I didn't bring Sam because he'll never understand the love a man can have for a place. There's no past and no future to Sam, only the present. But you know what was here before. I've listened to you tell Jamie about it. And now I look in your eyes and see the future."

"The future?"

"Old Yellow Shirt and I talked about it down at the old oak where we signed our treaty. He says this valley will know peace so long as you and Red Wolf ride the plains.

Well, I don't know about that. There's war and change on the wind, and things have a way of coming apart. But you're the one to make this valley grow and prosper."

Willie tried not to look at his father as the man spoke of the ranch, of the future. Anyone could tell he was saying good-bye.

Saturday night the horses were cleared out of the barn, and neighbors were invited to a dance in honor of the valley men who'd soon leave for the army. The company was a mixture of unmarried boys and older men who had someone to look after their families. One or two were as young as sixteen or seventeen.

Fiddlers were playing lively tunes, and corn liquor was making its rounds. Willie's mother had tried to keep him from coming, but Ellen Cobb was there, and the two of them were never apart when it came to barn dances and church socials.

Ellen was a spindly girl, with skinny legs and only the hint of a woman's figure. But there was life to every inch of her. She could dance down a grizzly bear, and more than once she'd raced Willie and Travis through the river. She was a year younger than Willie, but as little children they'd been nearly the same size. Now that Willie was growing, she liked to remind him how she'd outwrestled him when they were younger.

As they danced that night, Willie forgot about the war and his father's leaving. He forgot about the ranch and horses and cattle. He concentrated only on her face, on the lovely dark hair with streaks of red to it.

Her sparkling eyes danced along with the music, and as

they moved through the promenade, he felt something stir inside him. He noticed how she smelled of lilac, how her hands seemed to press right through his all the way to his heart. It was like he was on fire.

"Are you all right, Willie?" Ellen asked as he grew pale. "You're not faint, are you?"

"I'm fine," Willie said.

"Then pick me up, and let's get this dance moving," she said, tossing her hair back as she laughed.

Willie had no trouble lifting Ellen's frail body, then turning with the others to form a square. But when the fiddlers ended the song, he began leading her away.

"Let's walk awhile," Willie said. "The stars are nice this time of year."

"I'll go, but not for too long," she said. "Ma doesn't trust you, Willie, not after your time with the Indians."

"You figure I might take to some savage conduct, huh?" he asked, laughing. "Murder, perhaps, or worse," he added, grabbing her shoulders.

"Stop it," she said, pulling away.

"Are you afraid of the dreaded Comanche, Bright Star?" Willie asked. "I've killed my buffalo, been marked by the lance. All that's left for me to be a full-fledged warrior is . . ."

"Now you hold on right there, Willie Delamer," Ellen said. "I won't be laughed at."

"I'm not laughin'," Willie said, suddenly growing serious. "I think maybe I'm gettin' the notion to kiss you, Ellie."

"Don't you dare!" she said, retreating. "I'm not near old

enough for such carrying on. If Ma was to find out, and she would, Pa'd be after you with a shotgun."

"There'd be worse fates than married to you, Ellie," he said, trying to keep his face from turning crimson.

"It's not marriage but murder that'd be on Pa's mind," she said. "We've both got a lot of growing to do yet. In a few years, maybe . . ."

"You've thought on it, too, haven't you?" Willie asked. "I'll have the ranch one day. We could raise a fine herd of . . ."

"Herd?" she asked. "I'll not raise a herd of anything. Cattlemen! Got to think of children as a herd."

"I wasn't thinkin' about children," Willie said, the red finally taking over his face. "I was speakin' of horses. But there'd be children, too, as many as you wanted."

"I believe you're proposing to me, Willie Delamer," Ellen said. "Have you been into the corn liquor?"

"It's nothin' but the intoxicatin' nature of your smile, ma'am," he said, bowing to her.

"Why, Willie, you're a poet," she said. "I can't believe what's got into you. I always thought the only thing romantic to you was your love for those old cliffs."

"I'm just a cavalier at heart," Willie told her. "I'm a soldier of fortune seekin' the heart of the one I love."

She laughed, and the mood was lost.

"You're acting like a homesick calf," she said. "We'd best get back inside."

Willie frowned and followed her back to the barn. He felt like he'd just stumbled down a flight of stairs.

There was a buzz of excitement inside the barn. Men were signing a roster book and getting kisses from the ladies left and right. Travis pulled Willie off to one side.

"You hear the news, Willie?" Travis asked. "The men of the county decided to offer a good horse and twenty dollars gold to anybody who'd sign on with the regiment. How's that sound?"

"Like Papa's goin' to be out a lot of horses," Willie said.

"No, I mean to you? How 'bout joinin' up?"

"Are you?" Willie asked, his forehead all wrinkled.

"Thinkin' on it," Travis said. "They sure don't need me at home. And they say we'll be back in time for summer plantin' next year."

The two of them walked over and watched men file by and sign the book. Willie stared at his brother Sam, expecting the young man to move forward. Finally Bill Delamer himself walked over and stood beside his eldest son.

"Sam, we'll have need of a lieutenant for these men," the colonel said. "Will you serve?"

"Papa, I'd be pleased to serve in your command, but you know Helen's with child again. I can't leave her now. I'll raise a company of cavalry and follow you in a year's time."

"War'll be over by then," someone whispered, and there were many frowns among the people in the barn.

"Man can't choose his sons," someone mumbled.

Willie glanced at Travis a minute.

"You serious about joinin' up?" Willie asked.

"More'n a little," Travis said.

"Then let's go," Willie said, marching past his brother to the book and picking up the pen.

"Hold on there a minute," Willie's father said. "You're no more than a boy, Willie."

"Just this mornin' you said yourself I was a man," Willie said, writing his name, William J. Delamer III, in the book. Travis signed it then, and the two young men took their money.

"Willie?" he heard his mother call out.

"Sir, I'd be honored if you'd keep this," Willie said to Judge Taylor, returning the money. "Nobody ever had to pay a Delamer to do his duty."

There was a loud cheer, and several of the others returned the gold as well. The fiddlers picked up their bows and played a stirring version of "Dixie." The singing could be heard for miles.

Hours later as Willie lay in bed, the door to his room cracked open, and his father walked in.

"Willie, I wanted you to stay," his father whispered. "I left everything that's important to you in trust—my home, my family, this valley, the future."

"Papa, Tom and Sam are older, and they know more about runnin' a ranch than I do," Willie said, looking up at his father.

"They don't understand," the man said. "Tom's a carpenter, and Sam, well, after tonight I don't like to think what he is. You only signed the book because he refused."

"It's better this way. Sam's got his little ones, and I'm more of a fighter. I'm better suited to war."

Willie sat up as his father came closer.

"I won't lie and say I'm not proud of you," the man said, touching Willie's shoulder. "Nor will I say it won't be a comfort to have you at my side. But I wish you were staying."

"Papa, I'm a Delamer, too," Willie said. "And Delamers always stand in the first line."

Willie thought he saw a tear in his father's eye, and the big hand that moved across Willie's chest was soft in a way they'd both near forgotten.

3

WILLIE'S MOTHER SAID LITTLE to him that next morning. But after breakfast when the others had gone their separate ways, she led him aside. Together they walked down by the river.

"You know how I feel about this soldiering, William," she said, using his whole name for the first time in months. "How could you walk up there and sign that book in front of everyone? They'll expect you to go now."

"I am goin', Mama," Willie said.

"No, you are not," she said. "Your father is going. That's enough of a sacrifice for one family."

"Mama, they all say we'll be back by summer. There's little sacrifice to it."

"Your father doesn't believe anybody will be back by summer, not even by next year. This war's been brewing for a long time, and one little battle won't end it." Her face was all red and puffed up, and she trembled with rage.

"Mama . . ."

"Willie, you've always been a wild child. Your father and I have never tried to pull in the reins on you. It's kind of like raising a thoroughbred. If you break the spirit, you ruin the horse. But now the wildness has taken over, and I don't know what to do. You're a good boy, Willie, worth ten of any other I've seen in this valley. But you hurry yourself. Don't be in such a wild rush to find your death."

She leaned on his shoulder and cried a few minutes. Then she pulled herself back and stared into his eyes.

"I suppose you are your father's son, Willie Delamer," she said at last. "Come home to me. You were great trouble coming into this world, and you owe your mother something."

"Mama, I . . ."

"Don't lie to me, Willie, and say you hate to leave. You can taste the adventure, you want it so much. Be careful, and see you say your prayers. I'll think of you when I see the cliffs and listen to the Indians chanting."

Toward afternoon Willie rode out to see Travis and Ellen Cobb. The Cobb ranch was only five miles or so south of the river, and there was a well-worn trail. When he arrived at the gate of the Cobb place, he felt the spirit of adventure fill his insides.

"Ready to ride some, Willie?" Travis called to him.

" 'Fore long," Willie said.

"I been tryin' my aim," Travis said. "You ever try to hit anything with one of these long-barreled things?"

"Mexican War musket?" Willie asked, taking the gun

from Travis. "Shot a deer once with one. Clumsy kind of a gun. Papa got himself two new Sharp's rifles last year. Light, easy to handle, but he'll leave them for the ranch. I figure the state'll arm us."

"I could sure do with one of them new repeatin' rifles I heard about, Willie. Seen one up at Fort Belknap."

"Well, I imagine we'll fill them Yanks full of holes with whatever's handy," Willie said.

"Suppose so," Travis said.

After dinner that night, Willie and Ellen walked alone along the crest of a small knoll fifty yards or so behind the house. The sun was settling into some low hills to the west, turning the whole horizon a brilliant shade of orange. As they watched the sky, a stillness settled in around them, and their hands joined.

"I'm not too pleased with you, I suppose you know," Ellen said to him. "Last night you practically steal me away. One minute you're proposing. The next thing I know you're enlisting in the army. I'm not surprised Travis is going, but you, Willie! You won't be sixteen till next year."

"January," Willie said. "And besides, we'll likely be back before next summer."

"You won't get to Houston before the end of October," Ellen said. "And there's training after that. They won't be marching you off to Virginia before spring."

"Then the war will probably be over before we reach the field," Willie said. "All your worryin' will be for nothin'."

"If you really believed that, you wouldn't go at all."

"I'm goin' because it's my duty," Willie said.

"Men and their duties," she said, kicking up some dirt. "Willie, I don't care about duty or heroes. I only know I've gotten used to you being around, and I'll miss you."

"No more than I'll miss you, Ellie," Willie said, touching her shoulder. "I'll think of you when the sun goes down. I'll write you, too."

"You'll be different when you come back," she said. If I asked, would you stay?"

"If I said yes, I wouldn't be Willie Delamer," he said. "You wouldn't want a man who hid from a fight."

"I want you," she said. "Now and always."

"Then I'll come back to you, Ellie. Maybe a little older, but then we could both get a little bigger. And when I get back, I'll build a cabin down the river, and we can be married. You can raise kids, and we'll run a few thousand head of cattle. Now what could be better'n that?"

She laughed at him a little, then surprised him by kissing him on the forehead.

"That's no way to kiss a soldier," Willie said, glancing over his shoulder to make sure Ellen's father wasn't lurking around with a shotgun. Then he drew her to him, and they kissed on the lips, one long, sweet joining of their affection that was awkward in its lack of experience, yet because of that innocence perhaps more fervent.

Willie went each evening to the Cobb house, and each time the leaving grew harder. Returning home the night before the journey to Austin, he felt terribly hollow inside.

The stars were brilliant, and the wind seemed to sigh to

him. Willie stopped along the river and tied his horse to a small mesquite. Then he scaled the spirit cliff and sat down beside the burial ground of the ancient inhabitants of the valley.

Willie had been there many times. He'd come there with Red Wolf the first year they'd joined the deer hunt with their fathers. He'd climbed up there before leaving home to join the Comanches the year before. Always Willie felt a closeness to the sky on that cliff. Always he felt near God.

Once Willie'd watched the old chief, Yellow Shirt, pray to the spirits for strength. The chief had stripped himself and cut the flesh of his arms. Willie did the same thing now, then walked to the very edge of the bluff.

The wind lashed Willie's bare chest, blowing drops of blood from his arms onto his chest. Below him the valley stretched out in the darkness, and he felt terribly alone. Then something seemed to touch his shoulder.

"I am here tonight alone," Willie said. "Just me, naked as I was born. Lord, look down on me and make me strong. Lend iron to my shoulders and make my hands steady. Give me the heart to do what I must, and watch over me in the hours of my peril."

The wind grew quiet, and Willie heard his voice sail off into the night. Looking overhead, the stars smiled down on him, and he felt warm.

"Help me along the path I must walk, Lord, and give me your protection," Willie prayed. "And if I grow worthy, help me come back home again to those I love. And guard them so that I'll have them to come back to."

He brushed back the hair from his forehead and listened to the night sounds. Everything grew quiet, and he felt himself tremble. Then his nerves steadied, and he felt older, more confident. It was as if his prayer had been answered.

Turning around, Willie wiped away the blood from his arms and chest and got dressed. Then he made his way down the cliff and mounted his horse. He slept well that night. And when morning came, he said his good-byes and rode out with his father.

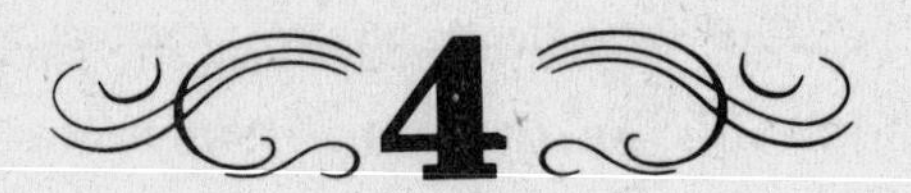

THOSE FIRST WEEKS in the army of the Confederacy were difficult ones. There was first of all the 250-mile journey to Austin, following the Butterfield stage line to old Fort Chadbourne, then across to the Colorado River and on to the state capital. On horseback the journey took two and a half weeks, and it was another week and a half on to Houston, where the rest of the regiment was being raised.

The chills of November were already in the air when the regiment reached Houston, and it was clear Ellen had been right. There would be no march eastward before spring.

It was far from an idle winter, though. Men were recruited, officers commissioned, supplies gathered, and weapons issued. Several hotels and two schools were appropriated for barracks, and a fine Houston lady named Mrs. Hazel DeLong designed a regimental uniform.

The Second Texas, as the regiment was named, would be the equal of any unit in the field. At least they would be as well clothed. Fine cotton trousers dyed powder blue with yellow stripes were added to gray tunics with buttercup cuffs and collars. Enlisted men bore chevrons of bright yellow, and officers had spirals of gold braid on each sleeve.

The city adopted the regiment for its own, and fine lots of smoked hams and sausages, fresh eggs and milk, sides of beef, and mounds of potatoes began arriving at the temporary barracks buildings. Never was an army better fed.

Willie worried, though. He heard his father mumbling about ordinance. The senators in Austin had promised a battery of cannons, and they were yet to be seen. New Enfield rifles from England were pledged, but instead crates of 1845 Mexican War muskets arrived.

"We'll take the field for God and Texas, but it's testing providence to fight Yanks with these old muskets," Tom Stoner said. "I believe these antiques might just blow up in a man's face."

Willie was amazed at some of the other soldiers. He'd fired guns all his life, but some of the clerks and wharf rats the regiment had drawn couldn't hit the side of a barn with a musket.

The officers and sergeants spent many hours correcting bad habits and poor posture. More balls were shot in practice than would have been needed to kill the whole Federal army.

Willie celebrated his sixteenth birthday at a fancy hotel with his father. The saber he'd asked for was refused, though.

"It's not proper for a private soldier to carry a saber,

son," his father had explained. "When you have need of one, I hope you'll carry mine."

Willie turned the weapon over in his hands with wonder. The beautiful saber had been cast in New Orleans for his grandfather. It bore the seal of the Republic of Texas on its scabbard, and the name Delamer was engraved on the blade. The saber had been lost at Goliad, but it'd been taken off a Mexican prisoner at San Jacinto and returned to Bill Delamer by Sam Houston himself.

When orders finally came for the regiment to report to Corinth, Mississippi, many tears were shed in Houston. The town's young women had grown attached to the soldiers, and a grand ball was arranged for the night before the regiment's departure.

No less a personage than Mrs. DeLong herself arranged the affair, and it was held at the manor house of a Mrs. Belle Davis outside of town. The great white house was smothered in flowers, and music filled the air. The ballroom was lit by wonderful chandeliers of fine crystal. Ladies in flowing gowns danced with gentlemen in expensive uniforms with polished brass buttons and sparkling sabers. An army of black servants in dinner jackets attended to every need, and there was laughter, singing, and cheering for the brave soldiers.

Willie had expected to go with the other soldiers, but his father arranged a ride in a long black coach. Walking up the steps to the huge mansion, Willie felt more naked than when he'd stood atop the cliff praying for courage. But his father's hand tapped him on the back, and he found himself relaxing.

Hanging over the balcony of the house was Mrs. DeLong's greatest creation, a blue silk battle flag with the seal of the old Republic of Texas surrounded by olive branches. It was the most striking banner anyone had seen, and together with the regimental standards sent down from Austin and the lone star flags carried by each company, it created quite a martial atmosphere.

There were bands playing and whole tables of food and drink. Willie followed his father past Mrs. DeLong and found himself face to face with a young woman about his age.

"William," his father said, using the name they shared for the first time in Willie's memory, "I'd like you to meet Miss Amy Carlisle, your cousin."

Willie looked at the face of the girl and recognized his brother Jamie's eyes. There was something about her nose, too. He smiled and kissed the young lady's hand.

"Would you do us the honor of entertaining Private Delamer this evening, Amy?" Mrs. DeLong asked.

"I'd be honored," the girl said, leading a bewildered Willie onto the dance floor.

"I'm afraid I don't know these dance steps, Miss Carlisle," Willie said. "I guess I'm more used to ridin' horses and shootin' buffalo."

"I imagine those things will suit you better in the days to come than would drawing-room conversation, Mr. Delamer," Amy said.

They looked at each other a minute, then laughed.

"Nobody calls me William," Willie said. "And certainly not Mr. Delamer. I'm Willie."

"And call me Amy," she said. "It does seem a little strange to be so formal with your own cousin. Now let me help you to the ballroom. Dance steps are simple for a horseman, and I'll make them easy for you."

Willie managed to stumble along through two dances before giving up. He led Amy out onto the veranda, and the two of them looked at the lights burning from the city.

"Do you own slaves, Amy?" Willie asked.

"Goodness no," she said. "Uncle Bill moved the family off a farm when he was old enough, and Mama has run a dry goods store ever since in Washington. My father is a county judge. Before I came to Houston to go to school, I'd only seen three Negroes in all my life. And they were freed men."

"I never saw a one till we started for Austin. I've seen many of 'em now, workin' in the fields or all dressed up like the ones here tonight. They don't seem so different from other men. Color's different, and their hair's curly."

"Oh, but they're suited to only the simplest of jobs, though," Amy said. "I haven't seen a one of them who could do figures or read and write."

"Well, I wouldn't know about that," Willie said.

The evening echoed with music and laughter, and it was hard to attend to anything that might be a serious subject. Willie took another turn at the dancing, and Amy led him around to meet her friends.

The ball finally closed when the musicians could play no longer, and even the ablest of officers had no strength left to dance. The men filed out of the great mansion and wandered back to their barracks. Soon many were asleep. But it would be a long time before the ball was forgotten. The beautiful women inspired greater thoughts of sacrifice among the men than a thousand battle flags and bands might have.

"War is such a grand undertaking," Mrs. DeLong said to Willie and his father that night. "It is the best that we can bring out in human nature."

Willie noticed that dark something in his father's eyes again. It was the only answer Mrs. DeLong received. But the pride and patriotism of the others outweighed it, and Willie couldn't help joining in the jovial singing and cheering the men of the Second Texas engaged in that night.

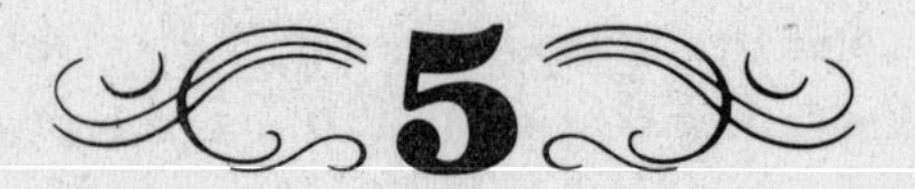

THE SECOND TEXAS MARCHED into Corinth the morning of April 1, singing the stirring words of "The Bonnie Blue Flag."

Hurrah! Hurrah! For Southern rights, hurrah!
Hurrah for the Bonnie Blue Flag that bears a single star!

Soldiers from Alabama and Mississippi lined the dusty road. The bearded veterans of the campaign cheered the newcomers and joined in the singing. And when the Texans sang "The Yellow Rose of Texas," a rousing cheer filled the air.

The men who marched into Corinth were not the same soldiers who'd left Houston, though. The splendid uniforms were coated with dust and worn from nearly seven hundred miles of forced marches. Half the command were barefoot, their boots victims of the swamps of Louisiana and the rocky trails of Texas and Mississippi.

While the colonel reported to General Johnston at his mansion headquarters, a staff officer ordered the regiment to encamp beside the railroad north of town. There were two other Texas commands in the army, but the Second Texas was assigned to Brigadier Jackson's brigade. The other three regiments were all Alabama units, with a battery of Georgia artillery thrown in for good measure.

Northern Mississippi had been turned into a quagmire by heavy rains, and the few tents that had survived the journey from Houston offered little protection and not a hint of comfort. Even so, Lieutenant Bales had the third company busy drilling before any one had a chance to catch his breath.

Old Tom Stoner, the grizzled veteran of the Mexican War who'd been made sergeant, hammered away at Willie and the others as if he were still in his Palo Pinto blacksmith shop. Just as Tom had once shaped a shoe for some tired old mule, he forged the clerks and cowboys of the third company into soldiers of the Confederate army.

As the men grumbled, old Tom frowned.

"The man who survives a battle is the man who knows his musket, boys," the sergeant told them. "I want those weapons clean and shinin', and I want you boys ready to answer a command!"

The grumbling subsided, and the soldiers turned their attention to the drill. The men had little thought for young Lieutenant Bales, the nephew of Mrs. DeLong, who managed to find a clean shirt in spite of all the mud. But for Tom Stoner, well, the men would follow old Tom to the gates of hell.

The drill continued until a little after noon. Rations were doled out then, and the men settled down to eat. Hard bread and bits of salted pork or dried beef were the staple of the army, with cold potatoes added in recognition of the hard march made by the Texans.

Willie found a tall oak tree and sat down beside Travis Cobb. They ate the meager supper together. A little later a cook came around with a bucket of chicory coffee, and each of the young privates dipped his cup into the steaming liquid.

"Feels good to have the day's marchin' done, huh?" Willie asked his friend.

"It'd feel better if the army could find me another pair of boots," Travis said, slipping one of the boots off his foot and sticking his fingers through the holes in the bottom.

Before the men could fall into their ranks and resume the drill, a great crash of rolling thunder shook the ground, and the skies opened up. Torrents of rain lashed the men, and soon the small white tents were crowded with soldiers.

Willie and Travis remained under the shelter of the oak tree, safely away from the leaky tents and musty odors of the other troops.

"We'd best find some wood and put together one of them shelters like the Alabama regiments," Willie said, pointing to the thatched huts across the railroad tracks. "Wouldn't take too long, and it'd sure be drier."

"You figure we'll be here that long?" Travis asked. "I

heard Captain Reynolds tell the lieutenant we'll be marchin' north any day now. Yanks're all spread out by the river."

"Well, I'm for stayin' here awhile," Willie said. "They've brought us this far. They can wait a week or so. It's for sure they're not haulin' any cannons through this mud."

"I don't know," Travis said. "They say General Johnston's a man of action. When he makes up his mind to fight, nothin'll hold him back."

"Nobody's done much fightin' in this army," Willie said, pointing to the scattered regiments that crowded the tracks. "We've got more vets in this regiment than in all them Tennessee and Mississippi units. Mostly these brigades've been fallin' back. I hear they lost Nashville without so much as firin' a shot. Now what kind of war is it when you give up a whole state just 'cause some army's marchin' around?"

"You'd've licked old Grant and his whole army, huh?" Travis asked. "Just walked up there and told him to put up his hands."

"I wouldn't've given up like them fellows at Fort Donelson," Willie said. "No, sir, I'd've fought awhile."

"They ought to make you the general, Willie. You got all the answers," Travis teased him.

"Trav, I never been one to be roundabout in my way of doin' a thing. If there's an army out there to fight, then we'd best fight 'em."

"Well, I don't know much about soldierin'," Travis said. "I guess I'm one to leave it to the general."

But the question of fighting or waiting did not limit itself to the two young privates. From the general staff on down, men argued about when and where to fight the next great battle of the western campaign.

"I heard we're on our way to Virginia in the mornin'," some Mississippi cavalryman shouted from his horse.

"No, we're headin' north to trap that Yank Buell at Nashville," someone else declared.

And there were reports from the cavalry scouts of Yank patrols less than fifteen miles away to the north.

"I seen their camps with my own two eyes," Willie heard a young-looking lieutenant say. "Tents spread out across a ridge so that you couldn't see the end of 'em. Must've been fifty thousand men there at least."

It was that report which disturbed Willie the most. He'd heard his father say how Buell's army at Nashville was on the move again, and soon they'd be facing a hundred thousand Yanks.

Willie couldn't even imagine a hundred thousand men. Walking around the army camps was enough to raise his eyebrows. Men were everywhere, huddled around fires and marching in line. Others were posted as pickets or busy washing clothes.

Mostly those days in Corinth were spent building shelters from the rain. Willie hadn't seen as much rain in a year along the Brazos as they'd had those first two afternoons and nights in northern Mississippi. The rains continued to flood the roads and dampen powder and everything else.

There was a lot of tension in the camps, and soon rivalries sprang up. Willie found the Alabama boys especially insulting, and even being outnumbered three to one didn't prevent some of the men from fighting.

"All they grow in Texas is snakes and cactus," a 'Bama corporal said. "I been there once on a trip to Santa Fe. And the women all look like pigs."

"I saw a 'Bama hog one time," Travis said then. " 'Course she was married to a fellow from the Nineteenth."

"Corporal, in fact," Willie added. "Saw her myself."

Pretty soon forty or fifty Confederates were tangled together, and only the prompt arrival of some Tennessee cavalry and the regimental commanders stopped the ruckus.

"Colonel, it would seem these boys are anxious for some excitement," Willie's father said to one of the Alabama officers. "Do you suppose we could arrange some more gentlemanly opportunity for their energies?"

"Seems to me we might race a horse or two, sir," the Alabaman said, a smile sneaking across his face.

And so they settled on a horse race. Soldiers lined up on both sides of the narrow road, betting the strange big bills still crisp from the Richmond printshop. The Alabamans had two fine white stallions and a chestnut gelding, all well-bred thoroughbreds from a stable in Louisville.

Lieutenant Bales offered his big long-gaited roan, but then Willie's father appeared with the big black Willie had ridden from Palo Pinto County.

"Let my son ride this horse," Colonel Delamer said to the men. "He might not be the fastest, but nobody gets out of a horse what Willie can."

"Hey, that boy ain't old enough to ride no horse," one of the Alabama privates yelled. "He ought to be home mindin' the cows."

"Just watch him ride!" Travis said.

"Ride him like old Yellow Shirt taught you, Willie!" Tom Stoner shouted.

Willie heard it all, but his attention was fixed on the tall black horse beside him.

"Boy, don't let me down now," Willie whispered.

The horse dropped his nose onto Willie's shoulder, and Willie freed his mind of everything. He looked up to the sky a minute, then took a deep breath. Closing his eyes, he said a brief prayer. Finally he threw himself onto the back of the horse and tore open his shirt so that the wind pricked the flesh of his bare chest.

"What's that crazy Texan doin'?" someone asked.

"Wait an' see," Travis told the crowd.

Willie urged the black over beside the others, and a staff lieutenant held up a red flag to prepare the riders. When the man dropped the flag, the riders took off.

Willie gritted his teeth and drove the big black onward. The other mounts were faster, but Willie rode the black as if the animal and rider were one and the same.

Amidst the dust from the road, little could be seen of the horsemen. Willie hugged the big horse's neck and pushed him on, urging the animal to be more than it was. And when a single horse and rider emerged from the dust, it was Willie and the Palo Pinto black.

The loudest cheer ever heard in northern Mississippi

came from that crowd of Texans. Willie turned the black, drew it to a halt, then raced back down the road, dropping the reins and riding Indian fashion between the rows of soldiers.

Another cheer went up, this time from the 'Bama boys, and when Willie finally halted the tall horse, he was met by a throng of men.

"Never seen anything like it," one of the soldiers said.

"That's what we call Texas horsemanship," Willie's father said, wrapping the young man up in his long arms.

"You made the boys some money, Willie," Tom Stoner told him as the men began settling their wagers. "No man ever took a Comanche Indian in a race."

"Well, I'm not a Comanche," Willie said.

"You rode with 'em for a whole winter," the sergeant said. "Far as I'm concerned, it's the same thing."

Travis walked over then, and the two of them took the big horse over to rub it down. As they worked on the animal, things seemed to have become simpler. Riding and handling horses took him back home, back to the Brazos that his heart had never left far behind. And as the night settled in once again, Willie didn't find his spirit dampened, even though the rains came again with all their fury.

6

Long before sunrise that next morning, Willie felt someone shake him out of his peaceful slumber.

"Willie, hurry and get into your uniform," Tom Stoner told him. "There's some captain from army headquarters out here. He's got orders for you."

"For me?" Willie asked. "There's got to be some mistake."

"Captains don't make mistakes," Tom said. "Not in the middle of the mornin'."

Willie dressed, then crawled out of the little shelter he shared with Travis and stood up. In front of him was a captain with the gold braid of a staff officer on one shoulder.

"Yes, sir?" Willie asked, giving the man a crisp salute.

"You're Private Delamer?" the captain asked. "I'm told you can sit a horse."

"Yes, sir," Willie said. "I been ridin' since I was three."

"Well, we've got a job for you, private. Report to army headquarters in one hour. And be ready to ride hard."

"Yes, sir," Willie said to the captain.

After the man left, Willie grabbed his rifle and saw that it was clean. Then he reported his orders to Lieutenant Bales and headed for the red brick house that served as the headquarters of General Johnston and the Army of the Mississippi.

"Private Willie Delamer reportin' as ordered," Willie said to a young lieutenant near the porch of the house.

"Delamer?" the lieutenant said, thumbing through some papers. "Oh, you're detailed for courier duty. Stack your musket, saddle a horse, and wait for orders."

"Yes, sir," Willie said, saluting again.

Willie stumbled around to the back of the house. There were two small carriage sheds there, one of which had been converted to a small stable. Other soldiers were standing around, and one of them helped him draw out a chestnut horse and slap a saddle on its back.

"You eaten yet?" a young man asked him.

"Not yet," Willie said.

"There's ham and eggs over by the fire," the other soldier said. "All you can eat."

"Thanks," Willie said, heading that way.

It didn't take long for Willie to make up his mind about the new duty. It was the first time since Houston he'd eaten fresh meat, not to mention eggs. And when a small black boy brought over a cup of steaming hot coffee, he thought for a moment he'd died and gone to heaven.

"Hard duty, huh?" the young man who'd spoken to him earlier said, sitting beside Willie on a small bench.

"You know, I could get to like this," Willie said.

"My name's Angus McLeod," the young man said. "Was with the Florida Batallion till yesterday."

"Willie Delamer," Willie said, shaking hands with the young man.

"Texas, right?"

"Second Texas Regiment," Willie said.

"Y'all just got here, right?"

"First of the month," Willie said.

"Well, we're glad you all are here, Willie," Angus said. "Wish you'd brought about twenty thousand more with you. Old Grant, he's got himself quite an army."

"What's this Grant like?" Willie asked.

"I heard they just 'bout took his whole army away, Willie. Then he went down to Donelson. He just up an' told them boys to quit, and their general went an' did it. Fifteen thousand men and the state of Tennessee, gone just like that."

"Well, we'll get old Grant and the rest of them this time 'round," Willie said.

"Don't you believe that, son," an old bearded sergeant said. "Yanks got themselves a fine army. Grant's a fighter. Saw him in Mexico."

"Why, you don't know an army from a horse's behind, Mitchell," another of the men said. "I rode right through that madman Sherman's pickets. Sat down with another trooper and had my breakfast right off a Yank's table."

"There's a lot of difference 'tween ridin' 'round through some Yank pickets on a horse and rammin' a whole army down them soggy roads," Mitchell said. "A deaf man could hear this army on the move."

Before the argument had a chance to continue, a major walked out and handed dispatch cases to most of the men. Only Willie and three others were left.

That whole day was spent standing around, waiting for orders of some kind. A thousand rumors floated around about when the army would move, but there was nothing to them. Willie returned to his regiment that night and went immediately to bed. Before he knew it, though, someone was stirring him to life.

"Willie, they've sent for you again," Travis told him. "They said to hurry back to headquarters."

"What time is it?" Willie asked, rubbing the sleep from his eyes.

"Close to midnight," Travis said.

As Willie got back into his uniform, he could hear the other soldiers mumbling to each other.

"If we do, son, you'll miss the sleep you're wastin' this minute," the sergeant said. "Now try to get some rest."

Willie knew as he left, though, that no one would get much sleep that night. He got to the small stable as fast as he could, and before he was fully awake he was carrying dispatches down the road to General Withers.

Always before, the messages had been folded in white envelopes, but these were sealed with wax. It didn't take an educated man to figure their meaning. It was clear they were marching orders, and it was all Willie could do to fight his curiosity and leave the seals unbroken.

All night the couriers rode. After the division commanders were alerted, the brigades and regiments received their orders. Willie didn't finish until half the night had passed. He finally slid off the side of his horse and collapsed in the soft grass behind the headquarters building.

A hand grasped his shoulder and stirred him to life that next morning.

"Soldier, are you ill?" a voice not unfamiliar to him asked.

"No, sir," Willie said, getting to his feet.

"They've had you riding hard, have they?" a tall man asked.

"Papa?" Willie asked, rubbing the sleep from his eyes.

"Colonel Delamer to you, private," the man said.

"Sorry, sir," Willie said, giving his father a stiff salute.

"I was only playing a bit of the devil with you, son," the colonel said. "I was wondering, Willie, if you'd walk a way with me."

"I have dispatch duty still, sir," Willie said. "I haven't been relieved, and they probably will have my hide for fallin' asleep."

"They can spare you a few more minutes after the night you've had," the colonel said. "Come along."

"Yes, sir," Willie said, following his father down the street a short way.

They stood together before the wide boulevard that faced the headquarters house. General Johnston himself stood with his staff on the porch, watching the lead regiments break camp and form up for the march.

"Will we fight soon?" Willie asked.

"Likely at dawn tomorrow," his father told him. "The general means to catch Grant in his camps before the rest of the army can reach him."

"Will Van Dorn's men be comin' into town today then?" Willie asked. "Someone said a message had come from them." There had been a lot of rumors flying around that General Earl Van Dorn from Arkansas was approaching with a Confederate army to reinforce Johnston.

"Van Dorn's not even close, son," the colonel said. "But we've got enough of an army here to make a fight out of it. I'd feel better with a fifth corps, but we're ready."

"We've got enough men to do the job," Willie said with confidence. "We can outfight any bunch of Ohio farmers that ever lived. Nobody from them Yank cities can shoot like a Texan."

"Willie, I'll tell you a little secret. When it comes to a battle, you'll find a man's pretty much a man, whether he's from north or south of the Ohio."

"Sir?"

"You get killed just the same by a Brazos cottonmouth as by a diamondback rattler. But that's not why I called you away from your post."

"Why did you, sir?" Willie asked.

"Oh, you might say I took to missing the sound of your voice, son. We haven't spent a lot of nights apart since you were old enough to notice. You know, Willie, I never had much time with my own papa."

"I know," Willie said, noticing a sadness in his father's eyes.

"I expected when you saw battle the first time that I'd be old and gray," his father said. "You're young to be a soldier. I joined the army myself at sixteen. I don't suppose I could hold you back from doing a thing I did myself. I do wish you'd leave this battle for me to fight, though."

"There's others in this army no older than me, Papa," Willie said. "And I've got a sharp eye with a musket."

"Willie, you keep in mind what I'm going to tell you. Keep your head down. Fire from cover when the opportunity presents itself. If the Yanks have cannons, keep yourself low to the ground. Mostly a cannon shell explodes a foot or two off the ground. And if they reach your line with a charge, fight like a cornered bobcat. Fight like there's no tomorrow, 'cause there isn't. If you act mean enough, there's those who'll leave you be. Understand?"

"Yes, sir," Willie said.

They turned away from the sound of men marching to war. Willie stopped when his father reached out and broke off the branch of a peach tree. He held it to his nose and smiled as the perfume brought back some memory.

"Spring's a good time to be alive," the colonel said.

"Best time there is," Willie said. "Sam'll be startin' the brandin' soon."

"I hope he's left with that cavalry company he was going to raise," the colonel said. "He might even be with Van Dorn."

"Yeah, Van Dorn," Willie said, sighing.

They both stared off toward Arkansas for a minute. Then Willie's father put a big hand on his son's shoulder and drew the young man to him.

"Willie, there's a thing I'd have you do for me," his father said.

"I'll do anything, Papa," Willie said.

"I'm not an old man yet, but I've seen the face of battle before. In Mexico they came close to killing me. Then there was old Yellow Shirt and his Comanches. If this is to be my time, son, I'd like to be taken back home, laid to rest along the Brazos with little Christine and Stephen. And I'd like for you to carry me home and stay there, look after your mama."

"They could never shoot you, Papa," Willie said. "Tom Stoner told me how one time the Comanches shot three arrows through you. You carried them arrows for twenty miles. Tom said you got off your horse half-dead, but the next week you were back fightin' Indians. They'll never get you."

Willie's father sighed a moment, then turned the young private around so that they stood face to face.

"You don't make it an easy thing to leave you, son. You ought to have a beard, a moustache at least. Your cheeks are just like a baby's," his father said, touching the side of his face. "You ought to be riding that big black of yours through the river, chasing Ellie Cobb around a barn and growing up. You've hardly got a trace of hardness to your whole self."

"I'm a soldier, Papa," Willie said, his face solemn.

"Well, Private Delamer, I leave you to your duties. Don't forget what I said."

"I won't, colonel," Willie said, saluting.

The two parted then, and Willie reported to the major in the orderly room.

"You boys can return to your regiments now," the man told them. "And don't take long getting it done. Some of the units are already on the march."

When Willie walked into the encampment of the Second Texas, Travis ran over to him.

"Willie, we've got orders," Travis said. "You'd best get your gear loaded up."

"We takin' it all?" Willie asked.

"Just a knapsack," Travis said. "Clothes and rations. Cartridges, too."

Willie began assembling his things in a knapsack. Before he was half finished, though, Tom Stoner shouted for him, and Willie ran out to locate the sergeant.

"Willie, the captain's lookin' for you," Tom told him. "He's got fire in his eyes, too."

"Captain Reynolds?" Willie asked.

"The very one. Now get over there," the sergeant said, shoving him along.

Willie reported to Captain Reynolds. The man was busy seeing the wagons loaded, but he stopped long enough to speak to Willie.

"Son, they want you assigned permanent as a dispatch rider up at headquarters. Soft life. You eat from the officer's mess, ride your own horse. What do you think?"

"I'd rather serve in my own company," Willie said.

"You'd what?" the man asked, his eyes full of surprise.

"I'd rather stay with the regiment, sir," Willie said. "I came all the way from the Brazos with these men, and I know my place here. I'm good with a musket, sir, and I won't let you down in a fight."

"Only a crazy man would turn this down, private," the captain said. "Or a brave one. I told your father I'd make you a corporal if you stayed, and he said you likely would."

"Corporal?" Willie asked. "There's lots of older men with more experience."

"Tom Stoner said you're the one he wants, and he's a good judge. Here."

Captain Reynolds handed over two fine yellow stripes, and Willie took them in his hand. Then the new corporal saluted sharply and ran back to tell Travis.

"Corporal Delamer," Travis said, watching Willie sew the stripes on his uniform tunic. "Next thing you know they'll make you a captain."

"Not till next year," Willie said, laughing.

A few minutes later the two friends stood side by side as their company formed up. Long lines were already filing down the road headed north, and Willie could hear the metallic rattle of the cannons behind their caissons. Soon the Second Texas was marching with them, marching toward the camps of the enemy not twenty miles away.

THE MEMORY OF THE LONG JOURNEY he had taken these last eight months left Willie as the fog settled in around the camp. But he was warmer with the remembering, and he found it possible to move away from the fire and walk down the road awhile. The cannons and wagons had made deep ruts, and thick black mud sloshed wherever he stepped.

Suddenly Willie heard the sound of horses on the road behind him, and he came to attention. Swinging the unwieldy musket around, he pulled back the hammer and prepared to challenge the intruders.

"Halt!" Willie cried out to the dark shapes emerging from the mist.

"We're Confederates," a man dressed in the uniform of a staff officer said. "What command is this?"

"Second Texas, General Jackson's brigade," Willie answered smartly. "Colonel Delamer's regiment."

"Heard any noise from the Yank camps?" the officer asked.

"A little singin' when the wind blows right," Willie said. "No patrols."

The officer, he was a major Willie believed, rode back to the others and saluted.

"All's quiet along the line, sir," the man reported.

"Move along down the line and check the pickets," one of the officers on horseback said. "I believe I'll stand by the fire for a time."

"Yes, sir," the major said, turning and heading back down the road past Willie's post and on to the advanced pickets of the right flank of the Southern army.

Four other riders followed the major, but the fifth, a tall man who seemed in charge, remained. The man rode his horse toward the fire, then dismounted with a grace Willie had rarely seen.

"I'll take your horse, sir," Willie said, grabbing the reins. "We've got a pot of chicory goin'."

"That would be kind of you, son," the officer told him.

Willie took the horse over and tied its reins to a wagon tongue. Then he grabbed the pot of chicory and poured a steaming cup of the stuff for the officer.

"Here you are, sir," Willie said, handing over the cup.

"Aren't you going to have some?" the man asked.

"No, sir," Willie said. "I can hardly tolerate the brew."

The man laughed, then handed back the empty cup. "Soldiering doesn't agree with you, I take it?"

"Well, sir, I don't know that it's supposed to be a thing

a man enjoys. But I suppose the food could be a bit better. We wouldn't feed some of this pork to a rattler back in Texas."

"Well, rations are hard to come by," the man said.

"I suppose," Willie said.

Several minutes passed in silence. Willie turned to watching the road, and the officer seemed distracted. Willie could tell the man's gaze was fixed on the ridge to the north, on the fires that marked the Federal campsites.

When Willie turned back to the fire, he was startled to notice for the first time the man's face. The man bore a grim look, but there was something familiar about his eyes. He wasn't as tall as Willie had thought at first glance. A trim brown moustache curled at each end, and long wavy hair fell over the man's ears. His hairline had begun to recede, but there was not a hint of gray.

"I'm sorry, sir," Willie said, coming to stiff attention. "I didn't recognize you."

"Nor I you," the officer said. "I've seen you before, at army headquarters."

"I was on courier duty, General Johnston," Willie said.

"You have a name, son?" the general asked.

"Delamer, sir," Willie said. "Willie Delamer."

"Not Bill's boy? I can see it now, in your eyes, I think. How old are you, Willie?"

"Sixteen," Willie said, wondering why that was always the first thing anyone asked him.

"Your father and I fought together in Mexico," General Johnston said. "And we fought Apache and Comanche Indians together before that."

"I know, sir," Willie said. "I've heard all the stories."

"I'll have to come take supper with you boys tomorrow when all this is finished with."

"We'd be happy to have you, sir."

"And maybe I can locate some real food for a Texas command," General Johnston said.

"That'd draw few complaints from the men, sir," Willie said.

"Come over and sit with me awhile, Willie," the general said. "You can watch the road as well from here."

"Yes, sir," Willie said, walking over and sitting across the fire from the general.

They sat there quietly for several minutes, staring at the fire with faraway looks.

"Tell me about Texas," the general finally said.

"You're from Texas, aren't you?" Willie asked. "What's to say?"

"There's always something to say about home, Willie. I never travel far enough to forget those hills of mine around Austin."

"That's nice country," Willie said. "We came through there on the way to Houston. It was fall, though. Papa said it's better in the spring."

"Flowers. I miss the flowers."

"There's not much about where I come from that'd make a man think of flowers," Willie said. "Cactus and mesquite, but not flowers. This is country for flowers. And peach trees. I've never seen so many peach trees."

"And magnolias. There's a sweetness in the air up here, but I wouldn't trade it for Texas."

"Me, neither," Willie said. "I like the river, the cliffs. You can hunt and fish and ride all day."

"You like horses, do you?"

"Love 'em," Willie said. "A man can let you down, but a horse'll run till his heart gives out."

"You ought to be in the cavalry, son," the general said.

"I know. I thought some about it just the other day, but the only Texas cavalry 'round here's the rangers, and they wouldn't take a runt kid like me."

Willie smiled, and the general laughed.

"General Johnston, what's it goin' to be like?" Willie asked, growing serious. "The battle, I mean. Is it hard to do, the fightin'?"

"No, you just look at your officer and do what he says. Willie, soldiering's not hard at all. The truth is, it's easier than lots of things a man does. You just see to it there's a good man on each side of you. Keep your eyes to the front and do your duty."

"I've seen men killed before," Willie said. "One of the hands got killed by a wolf summer before last. And I saw two Comanches ridden down by a buffalo stampede."

"Then you'll do better than most, son," the general said. "Sometimes I wish I was back carrying a musket in the line. A soldier can only lose a mile of ground. A general, though, can lose two whole states just writing a dispatch. And in a whole day's fighting he can throw away the war."

"I never looked at things like that," Willie said. "I still get scared, though."

"You're not scared, son," the general said. "Only wondering. Texans are born brave. Why, no other kind of a mule-headed fool would try to farm where a crow wouldn't fly, fight a thousand red Indians off a hill no rattlesnake would call home."

Willie spotted something of a smile in the man's eye. Then the major rode back up, and the visit was over.

"General, the pickets are set," the major said. "The attack is set for dawn. It's best we get some sleep."

"Watch yourself tomorrow, Willie," the general said, accepting a salute.

"Yes, sir," Willie said, getting the general's horse for him.

As the men rode away, Tom Stoner walked up with the two men who were to relieve Willie as sentries.

"Who was that on the horse?" Tom asked.

"Oh, just the general," Willie said.

"Jackson?" Tom asked.

"The general," Willie said, smiling. "Albert Sidney Johnston. He stopped by for a little of our chicory coffee."

"Willie, you can tell the stories," Tom said. "I'm goin' to have to stop talkin' 'bout my days in the Mexican War."

"It was General Johnston," Willie said. "He was settin' the pickets."

"An' talkin' to Corporal Delamer his own self," Tom said laughing. "Two yellow stripes and the boy gets generals talkin' to him. I hope to God they never make you a lieutenant."

"They're savin' that for you, Tom," Willie said, yielding his post.

Willie walked back to where Travis Cobb lay sleeping and rolled out two blankets. After standing there a minute amidst the stillness of the night, Willie slipped off his worn-out boots and looked at the sky. There were still no stars, and the chill returned to his bones.

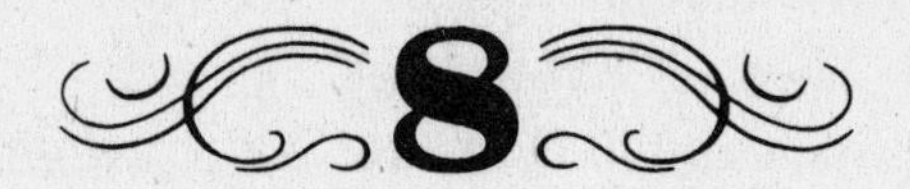

Dawn was still an hour away when the bugles sounded in the camps of the Army of the Mississippi. It was Sunday, the sixth day of April. The day had arrived that they had drilled and trained for these many months. It was the day of reckoning.

"On your feet, soldiers!" Tom Stoner yelled. "Come on, boys, rally to the flag!"

Willie sat up and rubbed his eyes. After yawning, he stumbled to his feet just as Tom kicked Travis hard in the backside.

"Come on, Travis, take your place," the sergeant said.

"Tom, ain't we havin' no breakfast?" a soldier asked from the third rank.

"Got no time for that," Tom told the man. "Better for belly wounds anyhow, they tell me."

The sergeant herded the rest of the men into line, then handed a roster of the company to Willie. As Lieutenant

Bales arrived with Captain Reynolds and Lieutenant Haller, Willie called out the names. Each man answered loudly, knowing it would be the final muster for many of them.

"Cap'n Reynolds, sir, do you have any words for the men?" Tom asked.

"Yes, I think I might," the company commander said, walking to the center of the hundred or so assembled soldiers. "Yes, sir, I might indeed."

Willie expected the captain to speak harshly. It was no secret the man believed his men were sluggish in drill and looked a little unkempt besides. But it was not with hardness that he looked down the line of soldiers. Finally the captain spoke.

"Men, we march to battle in a few minutes. I needn't remind each one of you how the honor of the Second Texas and the lives of your comrades rest on each man here. There are worse fates than death in battle. Each of us has someone back home praying for our safe and victorious return. I'd like you to take a moment and speak to the Lord. I know some of you don't like fighting on God's own day, but what we mean to do is strike a blow for Christian liberty and justice. I don't figure the Lord would mind us doing that on a Sunday."

Willie joined the others in a silent prayer, looking along the line of men and mentioning each one in his request for a safe return and a speedy victory.

"Now it's time to see what the Yanks are made of, boys," Captain Reynolds said. "Three cheers for the finest regiment in the Southern army!"

"Hurrah! Hurrah! Hurrah!" the men yelled, waving their hats in the air.

Willie's company fell in behind Captain Fredericks' command, and soon the entire regiment was marching toward the river in a column of fours. Ahead of them was General Chalmers' brigade, leading the whole corps in a kind of sweeping attack on the Federal center.

"We got the position of honor," somebody said. "Lead regiment of the brigade."

"Just means we got more likelihood of gettin' shot, if you ask me," another soldier said.

The column formation worked just fine so long as the regiment stayed to the roads, but as staff officers looked over maps and searched for a way to the front, men piled up, and commotion ensued. The subtle pops of muskets firing could be heard a mile or so to the left, and suddenly everyone was anxious to get into the fight.

"We've scattered their pickets, boys!" a wounded Mississippi boy called to the Texans. "Two volleys and them Yanks lit out for the Ohio."

There was a cheer from amidst the regiment, but Willie's eyes stared at the wounded man. Dark red blood stained the arm of a gray uniform, and by the way the soldier held his arm, Willie was sure a musket ball had shattered it. The surgeon would amputate most likely. That man would have but one arm for the rest of his life.

Willie judged it to be about six o'clock. The regiment had been on the move an hour, but scarcely half a mile had been covered. The road was still thick with mud, and the terrain around them was a tangle of briars and hickory trees. Occasionally the bright pink blossoms of a renegade peach tree lent color to the landscape. There were dogwoods as well.

As Willie followed the rest of his company along the road, he noticed a group of horsemen just ahead. General Jackson was there, together with Willie's father and some other officers. Captain Reynolds announced then that the regiment had been ordered to attack, and the men cheered.

"First to meet the enemy," Captain Reynolds said, waving the soldiers forward. "We're the heart of the right, boys. An army can hold with its left and center, but it strikes with its right!"

As the men crossed three treacherous creeks, though, it was clear most of the fighting was being done along the center. Federal pickets had been engaged in those fields, and Willie couldn't help staring at the scattered corpses in blue coats that lay along the road.

The Comanches that Willie had seen trampled by a buffalo stampede were just as dead as the Yanks beside the road, but the soldiers were different somehow. Their arms were thrown out in various directions, and one man had a large hole in his forehead. There was the smell, too, and Willie had to fight to keep his stomach down. Flies had begun gathering around the bodies.

Around seven the fighting grew heavy, and Willie looked on as his father spoke to General Jackson. There was a fork in the road ahead, and the Second Texas led the way to the right, followed by the Alabamans.

Navigating the thick brush was no small feat, and the

disciplined column of fours became hopelessly mutilated. Willie kept an eye on the men who should have been at his elbows, fighting the briars and tree limbs in an effort to stay close.

As the road meandered toward the river, Willie heard the heavy rumble of cannons, then the *pop, pop, pop* of muskets. A whole Yank brigade had been trapped in the attack, and Shaver's Arkansas brigade was teaming with Wood's six regiments in an effort to sweep the Federals back into their camps.

It was another hour before Willie's regiment finally formed for an attack. Chalmers' brigade was already engaged over on the far right, and there was a lot of talk about breaking though the Yank lines and racing for the landings.

"We'll have the whole Yank army trapped," Captain Reynolds said, waving his shiny saber in the air.

The Federals must have thought so, too, because they began a slow retreat, spreading out their ranks to the southeast. Supported by artillery, though, the Southern line charged, and the Yanks fell back further, fighting nearly in their own tents.

Willie could see nothing more of the battle. He watched Captain Reynolds ride through the thick underbrush, waving his sword and urging the men on down the narrow road toward the river.

The men tried to march in column, but soon the whole regiment was ensnarled. Men took their muskets from their shoulders and used them to fight back the brush. Men would pull back their hands, bloody from wicked thorns and jagged nubs left from limbs hacked away by bayonets. Behind them a dog barked from the edge of a field they'd crossed only minutes before.

"Where the hell are we?" Travis asked Willie. "You see the captain?"

"I can hardly see you," Willie said, stumbling over a log. Then two shots rang out, and a private ten yards or so behind them screamed out in pain and clutched his backside.

"They're behind us!" Willie said, turning to face the hidden enemy.

"Nobody's behind us but them blasted Alabamans," Tom Stoner said, threading his way through the soldiers, who had huddled in the shelter of a narrow ravine.

"Hold up there, you 'Bama pork-suckers!" Tom called out. "This is the Second Texas you've taken to firin' musket balls into."

"Hold your fire!" an Alabama major ordered as a volley near took the Texas sergeant's head off.

"You shoot at us one more time, you sons of horse manure, and we'll answer you in kind!" Tom screamed.

"It's them blue britches," the Alabamans complained. "That's all we can see."

The Texans eyed each other a minute. Before you could count to three, men were smearing black mud over the fine tailored trousers that only weeks before had been the pride of Houston's female population.

"That's not the place to catch a musket ball, Willie," Travis said, noticing all traces of blue were gone.

"Kind of hard to explain to the grandkids, huh, Tom?" Willie asked as the sergeant walked past.

"Boy like you, Willie, might not have none," Tom said, laughing.

"Let's get on the move here!" Willie heard his father's booming voice call out. "Texans move to the front. Come on, boys, let's get into the action. We ought to be sipping water from the Tennessee River by now."

Willie followed the others up a steep hill, trying to catch some glimpse of the battle through the heavy mist and the dense forest. It seemed, though, that for every ridge that was crossed, every creek forded, two were there to take its place.

The men were growing restless. The sun was climbing in the sky, and still the Second Texas hadn't tasted battle. It was humiliating to think of being mentioned in dispatches solely because one of the men had been accidentally shot by a nervous Alabama rifleman.

The men tramped their way down a hill, tripping on vines and stumbling along. Several men fell, tearing great gashes in their faces and hands. To one side the men could see Colonel Delamer conferring with General Jackson once more. Then the colonel rode down to the front ranks and began unraveling the regiment.

"Boys, the Yank camps are right in front of us!" the colonel shouted to the men. "You can see them blue-bellies eating their breakfast, too. Must be the middle of the morning. When you get across the creek, I want you to yell like wildcats and charge those positions. Keep your muskets primed and ready, but don't fire till you're on top of them."

Willie felt a stir among the men. At last they were to join the battle. At last it would be the Second Texas's chance to share in the glory.

"Get across that creek, boys, and wait for me," Captain Reynolds said, climbing down from his horse and splashing into the muddy water. "Ready? Let's go!"

The Texans howled and screamed like creatures from the world of the dead. The whole hillside was drowned in the noise. Suddenly a great gray wave started up the hill, shattering the morning stillness.

Willie stared in disbelief as the Yanks saw them coming, dropped their plates, and scattered. One or two found their rifles, but most headed for the other side of the world.

The charge of the Texans took Willie and his comrades across maybe three or four hundred yards of broken ground. Ahead of them lay a small road. Across the road lay rows of white tents, a whole regimental camp.

"Can smell them sausages, Willie," Travis said, running hard to keep up with the young corporal.

"First man to the tents gets furlough in Corinth!" Captain Reynolds yelled out.

"Corinth?" Willie asked. "We plan to be in Nashville tomorrow night."

The Texans closed to within a few hundred feet of the enemy when heavy firing broke out to the right. Men began dropping, but the charge didn't waver. Ahead Willie could see a Yank lieutenant getting his men into line to face the charge. Then Captain Reynolds gave the order to fire, and an accurate volley from the Texans staggered the Federal line and broke their resistance.

Willie and the others ran through the camp, shooting holes into enemy soldiers and taking close to a hundred prisoners. Out of breath from the hard charge up the hill, Willie fell to his knees and tried to catch his wind.

"It's not over yet, boys!" Lieutenant Bales shouted, pointing his sword at another Yank camp to their left. "Let's go get them!"

Willie couldn't believe his ears, but the lieutenant wasn't jesting. Just beyond the edge of the regimental camp they'd captured stood another. The rest of the brigade was already engaging it, but a Yank colonel was waving his sword in the air and rallying his command.

Just then the ground around them exploded with a volley of rifle fire, and three men fell to the ground mortally wounded.

"They've got those blasted new rifles," Willie said. "Let's get after 'em!"

With Lieutenant Bales leading, two companies of the regiment joined in a charge on the enemy position. The Yanks let loose a volley, shattering the Southern line. The Texans did not falter, though. Moments later they swept into the Federal camp, hollering and tearing into the Yanks.

Willie clubbed a Yank lieutenant with the butt of his musket, then stood on one knee and joined in a volley that struck down the Yank colonel and scattered his command.

Tom Stoner tore down the battle flag of an Ohio regiment, but most of the men taken captive were from the Fifty-fifth Illinois, refugees from the camp seized earlier by the Second Texas.

Willie lost his anger as he gazed at his enemies. Some hadn't had time to get their tunics on. Others stood in nightshirts and wept. Two young drummer boys no older than Willie's brother James glared at the Texans.

"They'll take you boys back to Corinth, I expect," Tom said, motioning for the prisoners to stand up. "We got to take your cartridges and all your weapons. But I'd allow as you might take some of that breakfast of yours with you."

Tom pointed to the food in the frying pans beside the Yanks, still hot. The Northerners nodded, then gobbled the food.

Willie turned and looked behind him at the face of the dead lieutenant he'd clubbed. Something shook him from deep within, and Travis grabbed his arm.

"You all right, Willie?" Travis asked.

"It's my brother-in-law, Trav," Willie said, pointing to the face of the lieutenant. "Tom Sheidler, Mary's man."

"No such a thing," Travis said. "Just a likeness is all."

But Willie couldn't stop his hands from trembling.

"Hey, come on, Willie," Travis said, pulling the young corporal away from the dead man.

"Just a minute," Willie said, kneeling beside the body. "I want somethin'."

Willie then reached under the dead man and pulled out a shiny new pistol. The hammer was still cold. It hadn't even been fired.

"Spoils of war." Willie said, stuffing the gun in his belt.

"I'd rather liberate some of that breakfast," Travis said. "Come on."

9

THE ROAD TO THE LANDING lay before them, and victory was that close. But it was impossible to carry on the attack. Some of the men hadn't eaten since leaving Corinth, and the Yank camps were a treasure house of cakes, breads, and all sorts of meat. Two whole barrels of salted pork were found, and the better part of a side of beef was located in a cook's tent behind the brigade headquarters. Eggs and bacon, jam and bread, fresh coffee and sweet honey were devoured by the hungry Texans.

Willie took a corner of dried beef and gnawed on it as he walked through the camps. He made his way among the dead Yanks, putting his foot beside each man in turn. The smell and the blood sickened him, but the run up the hill had turned the soles of his feet into giant sores, and Willie was determined to find some Yank shoe leather to solve the problem.

As he searched, Willie came up with something almost

as good, though. Under the body of a dead Yank sergeant was a brand-new Harper's Ferry rifled musket, the very gun he'd spoken of taking back to Corinth only a few days before. The sergeant's pockets were stuffed with bullets and a dozen or so cartridges. Willie helped himself to them.

Some of the Texans had discovered a sutler's wagon full of Cincinnati whiskey, and it was now being enjoyed. One young private had found four silk shirts in the tent of a Yank officer and borrowed them. Gold watches, gleaming swords, field glasses, woolen underwear . . . anything that was able to be moved was picked up and carried off.

As Willie passed a tent, something caught his eye. A reflection of some sort flashed in the sunlight, and he pulled out his revolver from his belt and walked over there. It was the buckle of a Yank bugler's belt. The man had been shot three times, and the front of his shirt was soaked with blood and gore.

Willie had seen many things in his months with the Comanches, but nothing could have been as horrible as the sight in front of him. His stomach revolted, but he looked away and breathed in the fresh air coming off the river. Somehow he managed to keep from being sick.

Looking back down at the young corpse, he nervously put his foot beside the man's boots. To his surprise it looked to be a near perfect fit. Taking a deep breath, Willie sat down and pried the boots off the dead Yank's feet.

"Heaven help me do this thing," Willie said, avoiding the terrible glance of the dead bugler. "They can't help you anymore, mister, but they'll keep my feet from gettin' peeled raw."

Willie exchanged his boots for the Yank's, noticing the fine heavy leather soles of the newer pair.

"Like as not you had a horse to ride," Willie said. "Thanks for the boots."

Then he got to his feet and made a fast retreat away from the dead bugler.

"You got yourself that rifle, didn't you, Willie?" Tom asked as he walked back to his company.

"Yes, sir," Willie said. "Got ammunition and everything."

"And a pistol to boot," Tom said, pointing to Willie's belt.

"Best of all," Willie said, tapping the heels of his new boots together.

"Willie, there's blood on them boots," Tom said. "You take 'em off a dead man?"

"Didn't figure he'd mind now," Willie said. "My old boots were near gone."

"I should've thought of that," Tom said. "Like as not there ain't any left that'd fit me now."

"You might get lucky," Willie said.

"Sergeant Stoner!" Captain Reynolds called out then. "Sergeant Stoner!"

"Willie, you see what he wants," Tom said. "I aim to scout out a pair of boots."

"Sure," Willie said, walking up the hill to where the officer was standing.

"Corporal, have you seen Sergeant Stoner?" Captain Reynolds asked.

"Yes, sir," Willie said. "He's gone to look for a new pair of boots."

"Boots?" the captain asked, his face turning red. "This is no time for chasing down boots! Get him!"

"I don't know as I could find him, sir," Willie said. "Maybe I'd do."

"Well, I suppose one man's as good as another. I've got about thirty prisoners back there," the captain said, pointing to a huddle of men in blue shirts sitting beside one of the big guns of the Georgia battery. "They need to be marched about three hundred yards to where General Jackson's set up an assembly area."

"Yes, sir," Willie said, saluting.

"And Willie, you'd best take care. Get five men you know can kill. One of the men heard them talking as if to plan an escape."

"Yes, sir," Willie said, surprised the man had called him by his first name.

Willie rounded up Travis Cobb and half a dozen others. The Texans got the Yank prisoners to their feet and began herding them back to the assembly area.

"Now you boys walk slow and take it real easy," Willie said, pulling out the pistol and firing it once about an inch from a big sergeant's toe. "I know how to use this piece, and I will."

"You killed lots of men, have you, Texas?" the sergeant asked.

"Three today," Willie said.

"He shot a cattle thief when he was eleven," Travis said. "Right between the eyes."

Willie tried not to laugh at the lie. Willie'd shot at the thief, all right, missing the man but putting a big hole in the rump of the rustler's horse.

"That's right," Willie said, rubbing his fingers along the cold barrel.

Willie turned the prisoners over to an officer from General Jackson's staff. As Travis led the way back to the captured camps, Willie stared at a cluster of Ohio infantry privates huddled under a tall oak tree. Willie saw nothing about those men that was different from himself. One of the Yanks noticed Willie's gaze, and the man waved.

"You boys from Texas?" the Yank asked.

"Brazos country," Willie told them.

"Hear they got prime horses out that way," the Yank said. "That right?"

"A horse off my ranch'll run all day and half the night," Willie said. "I rode one three days straight out near the Concho. Was half pinto, though."

"Half what?" the man asked.

"Pinto," Willie said. "Spotted kind of a mustang. The Comanches ride 'em. Fastest horse I even seen for a couple of hundred yards. You can race the wind on one of them."

"I'm from Kentucky," the Yank said. "Name's Jonas Phipps."

"Willie Delamer," Willie said. "This here's my friend, Travis Cobb."

"Travis," Phipps said, nodding.

"How come you to fight with the Yanks?" Willie asked. "Kentucky's a Confederate state."

"Nope," Phipps said. "Never left the Union. But I joined up with an outfit in Cincinnati. My two brothers are wearin' gray coats, likely on this field."

"You mean your own brothers are in the Southern army, and you're a Yank?" Willie asked. "That don't make sense."

"They got their feelings, and I got mine," Phipps told them.

"Such as?" Willie asked.

"Take slavery. I seen black men beaten half to death in Covington. I seen one had himself cut in half just for lookin' crosswise at a white woman. Don't seem right for a man to own another man, so I rallied to the cause."

"That's why you come down here?" Willie asked. "That's just close to the dumbest thing I ever heard. You know, I never even seen a Negro 'fore last fall. Never owned any, nor my papa, neither."

"Then why you come here?" Phipps asked.

" 'Cause I always figured what a man does is nobody's business but his own," Willie said. "I don't guess I like men ownin' other men any better'n you, but I guess maybe I wouldn't shoot somebody over it. But you Yanks wouldn't leave the peace be. Mr. Lincoln called out himself a whole army."

"Who fired on Fort Sumter?" one of the other Yanks asked.

"If a hornet was buildin' a nest inside your trousers, wouldn't you jump on it?" Willie asked.

The Yanks laughed, and pretty soon the argument faded.

"Tell me, Texas, you got yourself a girl back home?" Phipps asked.

"Yeah, but I can't talk on her," Willie said.

"How's that?" one of the others said.

"She's my sister," Travis said.

"I tell you what, though," Willie said, winking. "She's just about the prettiest thing you ever did see. Eyes like violets, and hair the color of chestnuts. Her skin's smooth like fine cotton.

"They all like that in Texas?" a tall Yank asked.

"Mostly," Travis said.

"We been fightin' for the wrong side, boys," the tall Yank said. "Let's join them Texans."

Willie laughed a minute.

"We'd better get on back now," he said, hearing the beat of drums from the captured Yank camps. "I'm a corporal, remember. It'd be hard for them to start without me. See you Yanks another time. Maybe they'll take you up to Nashville for the exchange."

"Nashville?" Phipps said, shaking his head. "You've got a lot of fightin' to do, Texas, 'fore you get to Nashville."

"We got time," Willie said. "We can give you Yanks a day to lose this battle. Maybe we'll take a whole week to capture Nashville."

"That's longer than it took you to lose the place," one of the other Yanks said. "We'll be seein' who holds what ground 'bout this time tomorrow."

As Willie and Travis headed back to their regiment, they talked about the fighting which lay ahead.

"It doesn't matter if the whole Yank army's waitin' for us," Willie said. "We can take anybody. We're the Second Texas."

10

SURE ENOUGH, THE REGIMENT was re-forming. The Federal army had thrown half a brigade of reinforcements in a gap between the shattered remnant of the brigade that Chalmers was pressing on the Yank left flank and the strong position the Yanks were manning along the sunken road.

It would be no Sunday hayride this time. Three Illinois regiments had taken up a line atop a ridge. To get at them the Southerners had to cross a deep ravine and scale the hill. Some intense artillery fire was coming from a battery of cannons back of a lovely orchard of peach trees.

"Move the men up," Willie heard his father say grimly. "Hug the ground, boys. Get as close as you can, then run like madmen."

Willie could tell from his father's tone that there wasn't much chance of running these Yanks back to the river. Even as the Terxans were approaching the ravine, the field in front of them was raked by fierce fire from the rifled muskets of the enemy, and more than a few men fell dead.

Following the volley, the Second Texas and the Nineteenth Alabama swung to the right, and the other two Alabama regiments joined another brigade to attack the ridge straight ahead. The Texans moved forward through tangled undergrowth and deep cuts of earth. The ground gave way from time to time, and men stumbled and fell, only to rise and be hit by rifle fire or fragments from shells fired by distant cannons.

"Let's go, boys," Lieutenant Bales cried out, running in front with his sword flailing away at the air.

The next Yank volley blew the lieutenant's body apart, and the Texas regiment froze.

"Get down, boys!" Tom Stoner yelled as the sharp fire cut down another dozen soldiers.

"There's no way to get up there," Willie said, crawling along. "We'll lose half the regiment 'fore we get halfway."

"And the rest from there on in," Travis said.

"Let's go, Texans," Captain Reynolds said, walking over. "Let's take that ridge!"

"Sir, they've got us pinned right where we are," Tom Stoner told the man. "Lieutenant Bales was out there two seconds before they spattered him all over the place."

The captain glanced at the corpse of the other officer, then swallowed. "Boys, we got to take that ridge," he said. "What I aim to do is this. We're going to move out two steps, then fall back. Soon as they fire, run like hell about a hundred yards, then fire. Likely we can put some holes in them for a change."

The men nodded at the plan, and it was settled. When the captain waved his sword, the men leapt forward, then fell back. It disturbed the aim of the Yanks, and their volley was wild. Even so another fifteen men went down.

"Let's go," Tom screamed, waving the soldiers onward.

Willie hollered, too, and the cry of several hundred Texas fanatics was unnerving. Even the Alabamans to the left seemed shaken. Up the ravine went the regiment, in spite of withering fire from the ridge, in spite of shells crashing into their ranks from the guns behind the Peach Orchard.

When the Texans pulled to within several hundred feet of the crest of the hill, they halted. Every musket and rifle swung level, and a fierce volley tore into the ranks of the blue-coated soldiers ahead of them. The Federal line wavered, and when the Texas charge resumed, the whole enemy line pulled back seventy-five yards or so and struggled to re-form.

From the top of the ridge, the Confederates controlled the high ground that had anchored the entire Federal line. The meager remains of the enemy brigade near the river were put in a hopeless position, and what was left of the two regiments there simply melted away, falling into the hands of Chalmers' Mississippians or drifting back to the landing. But they could hardly have been called a brigade anymore.

The Union guns that had been firing on General Jackson's attack pulled back about fifty yards to protect the flank of the Peach Orchard, and the Southerners leveled a murderous fire on the three Illinois regiments below them. Willie found it much like shooting squirrels back home. More than one Yank fell stricken by a ball fired from the new rifled musket.

It was getting close to midday, and the regiment had shot up two-thirds of its ammunition. Captain Reynolds told the men to hold their fire, then left to find the colonel.

"We need to send someone back to the supply train for powder and shot," the captain said. "The men are down to only three or four shots apiece."

"Tell them to hold their ground a few minutes," the colonel said. "Then we'll see what we can do to that line with three hundred bayonets."

"Bayonets?" Travis asked. "With them shooting rifle balls at us, we're chargin' with bayonets?"

"It might work," Willie said. "They won't expect a naked charge."

"You're right about that," Travis said. "Not even a fool charges three regiments without any shot for his musket."

Willie saw his father halt a few minutes and gaze down the thinned ranks of the regiment. It took little time to notice some old friends were among the missing. Willie moved back and glanced up at the colonel. The man sat a different horse, a tall white stallion with a Yank saddle.

"Papa, don't you think we could send somebody back to the wagons?" Willie asked.

"Son, we've got regiments and brigades scattered all over the countryside," Willie's father said. "God only knows where our train is. Most likely still in Corinth. There's no time for any more waiting. We have to hit while they're confused. Those boys on that ridge are nervous, and another charge will move them."

"Yes, sir," Willie said, saluting.

"Willie?" the man asked.

"Yes, sir," the young corporal answered.

"Remember what I said, son. Keep low to the ground, and fight like a bobcat."

"I will," Willie said.

As the Texans prepared to mount their attack, a strange ringing sound was heard from in front of the Eighteenth Alabama's positions. A great roar of laughter erupted from both sides of the line, and soon the Texans joined in. A sort of unofficial cease-fire ensued as a family of goats, two big nannies and a huge billy, followed by three little ones, trotted along in a carefree manner between the lines.

"Hold your fire!" Captain Reynolds hollered.

"Cease firing!" a Yank major commanded.

For several minutes silence hung over the battlefield, disturbed only by the twinkling sound of the bells that hung around the necks of the goats. Then a bold young Yank captain jumped his horse over the bluecoat line and rode out in front.

"Gentlemen, I accept the surrender of these goats in the name of the United States of America," the captain called out. "I assume you will not protest the assistance we will give to these unarmed civilians?"

The billy goat raised its hind legs and stirred up quite a protest among the Confederates.

"Sir," Willie's father said, "you can surely see these fine Confederate goats are merely seeking the safety of my lines. Kindly let them pass."

There was a rousing cheer from among the Texas soldiers, and one of the little goats made a bold run into the safety of the Confederate positions.

"I must insist you yield these civilians to me, sir," the Yank major said.

The goats again protested, and one of the nannies and the other two small ones raced across the field to the safety of the Southern lines.

"I'll shoot the next goat that moves to join you rebels!" the Yank captain screamed, drawing his pistol.

"Then I'll shoot you!" an Alabama private yelled.

The major took two steps toward the billy goat, and a shot rang out that blew the man's hat off his head.

"He's a secesh goat for sure, major!" the captain called out. "Cover me!"

The Yank captain returned to the safety of his lines, and the Confederates pleaded for the last two goats to come across the lines. Finally two rifle shots split the stillness, and the nanny goat spun around, blood covering her mouth and side.

The big billy then turned and raced for the Federal line, butting and annoying the Federals until one of them put a bayonet through the goat's chest. Silence settled over the field a moment, and then the whole Southern line surged forward. Screaming like wildcats, the force of the charge shook the ground, and the Illinois soldiers froze. Some managed to get off a shot. Others dropped their rifles and fled.

The charge of the Texans was savage. Bayonets flashed in the sunlight, stabbing through soft flesh and shattering limbs. Hideous cries of the dying, moans of the wounded trampled under the feet of the charging Southerners, and terrifying screams of victory all joined in to create a scene out of hell. Wild-eyed soldiers fought and killed and died until the hillside ran with blood. When it was over, the whole of the Union left was falling back in chaos past the Peach Orchard, and the Federal center was in serious danger of being flanked.

The Second Texas lost over a hundred men in the attack, including Captain Reynolds, and the unit was reduced to half its original strength. Out of ammunition, shot to pieces, its survivors already having made three hard charges, the regiment was worn out. But when General Jackson rode up, Colonel Delamer saluted and reported the regiment full of fight.

"Bowen's ready to make another run at the Yanks behind those fences," the general said. "Bring your regiment around in support. Be ready to charge their flank."

"Yes, sir," Colonel Delamer said. "We'll fight 'em in Memphis if we're asked."

What was left of the regiment moved across the battlefield like scavengers, taking every weapon that could be found, especially the new rifled muskets. The men soon re-formed in a line of sorts, and the regiment moved out behind the Alabama units in the direction of the Peach Orchard.

Willie looked around at the thin ranks of his company. There were no officers left, and Tom Stoner was the sole surviving sergeant.

"Not many left, huh, Willie?" Tom asked, reading the young man's thoughts. "This Tennessee land don't come cheap."

"No, there's a high price to it," Willie said.

"You know you're second in command now, don't you?"

"Second in command of what?" Willie asked. "I count twenty-three men out of a hundred and five we started with."

"Well, we've led the attack," Tom said. "Front line always gets cut up some."

"I seen a wolf chew a chicken before, Tom," Willie said, trembling. "But there were men back there cut up worse. Men blown to pieces so you wouldn't know 'em."

"What'd you expect, Willie?" Tom asked. "Men die a lot of ways in a battle. Not many get it quick and sudden through the head. I seen a man shot in the belly who lasted a whole week, coughin' blood and yellin' for water."

"Water?"

"I couldn't give it to him, Willie," Tom explained. "It would've made the pain terrible."

"What'd you do?" Willie asked.

"I didn't stay around him much. He died. If they got me in the belly, I'd grab a pistol and shoot myself. I don't never want to see myself goin' like that man."

Captain Fredericks got the men into line and pointed to the Federals who were frantically forming a line in front of the Peach Orchard. There was a commotion then to

Willie's left, and the men glanced around in time to see several riders moving forward.

"It's General Johnston!" someone yelled. "He's come down to lead the charge himself."

"Hurrah!" the men of the Second Texas yelled.

"Hurrah!" the Alabamans echoed.

Soon cheers were enveloping the whole Southern line. The general himself had come to lead the charge that would shatter the Union left and allow the final blow to be dealt Grant's army. Willie looked back from his high perch on the edge of the ridge at the wide waters of the Tennessee.

"Supper in Grant's tents," he whispered.

And then the men began moving forward.

11

General Johnston was mainly occupied with getting two brigades from the reserve corps formed for direct charges on the Peach Orchard, while Willie watched his father and General Jackson try to regroup the brigade for its supporting attack on the Union left.

"Would you look at that," Travis whispered, pointing to General Johnston riding his horse in the midst of an intense fire from the orchard. "I'd follow that man anywhere, Willie."

Willie knew the feeling. There was something about a fearless officer that drove a man. It was like the general was immune from harm. All around the man soldiers were dropping. Officers fell from their horses. And still the general rode along the line, calmly giving orders and preparing the men for the charge.

When everyone was in position, the officers raised their sabers and waited for a signal. When the general gave it, the sabers dropped, and the men eagerly raced across the orchard. Willie's regiment, with the rest of Jackson's brigade, ran through the trees to the right, howling and screaming, ready to destroy the Illinois regiments in their front once and for all.

The force of the Confederate attack was incredible. In spite of a staggering volley from the Federals, Willie and his fellow Texans drove through the enemy ranks like a Texas cyclone. Bayonets flashed. Men fell. It was the ridge all over again, except fifty times over.

The whole battle was practically on top of the Hamburg and Savannah Road, and most of the Union soldiers just took to the road and ran toward the rear. Some didn't even bother to take their guns, just lit out like jackrabbits.

Willie felt his legs give way, and he stumbled to the ground. His hand sunk into something wet and sticky. Looking down, he saw the ground was literally covered with blood. He got to his feet and walked over behind a tall hickory tree. There he vomited until his head was light and his stomach empty.

"God, this can't be real," Willie whispered, blinking his eyes.

Somehow he expected it all to fly away. He thought any minute he'd wake up in his warm bed back in the small white house above the Brazos. But the smell of death hung heavy in the air, and he could tell this was no dream.

Looking to one side, Willie could see men half blinded by powder flashes stumbling blindly across the hillside. Wounded soldiers lay everywhere, calling out names of sweethearts and friends, wives and children and mothers. Tom Stoner was busy getting the wounded moved off the road.

"Don't you worry, boy," Tom told a wounded private. "They'll be comin' for you 'fore long."

One side of the road was filled with Confederates, the other with Federals. Some of the men went around with canteens and offered the wounded drinks. Men with stomach wounds were screaming out for water, and some of the soldiers fought back tears as they refused those dying wretches their final request.

"I worked in a slaughterhouse when I was fourteen," a soldier on Willie's left said. "Never saw anything like this, though."

Limbs were hacked off. Pieces of people rested everywhere. The foul stench of dying men mixed with gunpowder and the hot Tennessee sun to form a nauseating combination. Willie suddenly felt an impulse to turn and run, race all the way back to Texas. He wanted to wake up from this nightmare. But his father's words calmed him.

"Boys, they're having a time of it over to the left," the colonel said. "Let's see if we can't give them a bit of a surprise."

Captain Fredericks took command of three companies, close to a hundred and fifty men, while another group about that large followed Willie's father and one of the Alabama colonels toward the Peach Orchard.

Confederate cannons blasted holes in the thin blue line, and the Texans and Alabamans hit the Federal flank. Gray-clad Southerners swarmed over a low fence, forcing the fleeing Yanks back into a tangle of woods behind a small cabin.

The rest of the Alabamans began forming a new line north of the Peach Orchard. A terrible blow was delivered to the army then. A youthful-looking Tennessee bugler rode over to General Jackson and delivered the news. General Albert Sidney Johnston was dead.

"Just can't believe it," Travis said, sitting down and putting his face in his hands. "The commanding general."

"I was just talkin' to him last night," Willie said, turning to Travis. "Trav, he was tellin' me how hard it was bein' a general. Well, I guess it's as easy to die as a general as it is when you've got two yellow stripes on your sleeve."

Willie coughed, then wiped a tear off his cheek. He hadn't cried since his little brother Stephen had taken a fever and died six long years before. He didn't think generals would want tears, so he swallowed his sadness.

As the men sat around sobbing and praying, horses trampled down the road, and Willie spotted his father.

"Form up, men!" the colonel shouted. "It's time to move along. We're marching to the sound of the guns."

"It's for sure it's the sound of somebody else's guns, colonel," Tom Stoner said. "We've nary ten cartridges amongst us."

"There's more coming," Captain Fredericks said, riding up behind the colonel. "Get your company formed, sergeant."

It wasn't hard to gather the third company. Only about

twenty men were left. The rest of the regiment was better off, there being two hundred sound men or so left in all.

"I'll wager we've lost half the command," Willie heard his father tell Captain Fredericks. "Major Denard took a ball through the arm, and they're patching him up. The lead passed through, so he should be with us by three or four o'clock."

Willie frowned. There weren't but seven officers left in the regiment. The way the fight was going, they'd all be dead before nightfall. Led by their colonel, though, the men moved on down the road in a column of fours, only to stop a few hundred yards ahead as dense smoke from the burning forest behind the sunken road blocked the way.

A small pond stood there, and the thirsty men raced for it. Some jumped in. Others just bent over to quench their thirst.

There was a cooling effect to the water, and Willie wet his kerchief and washed the powder and smoke from his face. His head cleared, and he walked to a small knoll and sat down. Right then there was something terribly wonderful about being alive, and he found himself laughing.

"It's kind of crazy, isn't it, Willie?" Travis asked. "Killin' Yanks, them killin' us. All of us chargin' across this Tennessee farmland."

Willie didn't answer. There was no more laughter inside him. His eyes were fixed on the waters of the pond. And something was filling his brain, tearing at his insides.

12

BLOODY POND the soldiers called it. As more and more wounded crawled their way to the banks of the pond, the water began taking on an appalling brownish tint. There were even those who collapsed along the bank and fell face first into the water. If nobody pulled them out, those men would sputter and drown in the shallow pond.

All the horror of war was visited upon the men who sat around that pond. In the woods just a few hundred yards away the Federal line was struggling to re-form, and one battery of guns was opening up on the Confederates.

"Form up!" Tom Stoner yelled, screaming at the top of his lungs. "Second Texas, close ranks!"

Willie and Travis made their way to Tom's side, and the men knelt and fired a volley into the woods. The guns grew silent a moment, and the soldiers paused to catch their breath.

On a small rise of ground behind the thin line of Southern soldiers stood several officers on horseback. Willie recognized General Jackson, the brigade commander, and General Withers, who commanded the division of Bragg's corps that included the two brigades on the far right of the Confederate army.

The tall general in the center was a stranger to Willie, but not to Tom Stoner.

"That's General John C. Breckenridge, Willie," the sergeant said. "'Bout a year back he was vice president of the whole country."

Willie remembered the name. There'd been a lot of Texans who'd voted for the man to be president, his father among them. General Breckenridge commanded the reserve corps, and he seemed to be taking charge of the right flank. Things were pretty confused, what with General Johnston dead and Beauregard, who was senior in rank, somewhere to the west.

There was a lot of heavy fighting around the Yank center, and a couple of batteries had been pulled over to the far right where somehow the scattered troops there had pulled together for one last stand. The firing there didn't last long, though, and soon the troops from Chalmers' brigade began moving over to take their positions alongside the Second Texas.

"Never saw a thing like it," one of the tough old veterans of the Fifty-second Tennessee told the Texans. "Line of Yanks runnin' across them ravines like a bunch of scared rabbits."

"Was like shootin' squirrels in a creek bottom," another Tennessee boy said.

"I seen fifty go down in one volley," the first man said.

"Those boys fought well," Tom Stoner said. "They held the whole right side of our attack for most of a day."

Willie respected those who'd stood and fought, too, but he couldn't bring himself to think about it. There was a danger in feeling anything for your enemy. He'd seen a good man's aim spoiled when he got soft on a deer. In a battle, a soft spot could get a man killed.

Once Chalmers' brigade was aligned with Jackson's men, General Breckenridge ordered the line forward, to the edge of what Colonel Delamer called the Wicker Field. The Confederates began forcing the Federal line back into the woods.

There was a roll of drums all along the line, and the cavalry along the far right of the Southern line stirred to a blast of bugles. Willie and the rest of the Texans emerged from the woods to find themselves in the midst of a field. Along the road stood a small cabin, filled with wounded soldiers from the fighting earlier in the Peach Orchard. The Union line had formed in depth in that field, and soon a withering fire enveloped the whole of the Southern position.

Willie watched as the men in the brigades to each side of them lay down on the ground and fired away at the Union line. The Second Texas, almost out of ammunition again, was moved aside some, leaving the three Alabama regiments to form the main front.

An exchange of volleys shook both lines, and neither side was able to gain ground on the other. The Federals then brought some cannons to bear, and shells started falling among the Confederates, fired from far behind the trees that cropped up at the edge of the field.

Not to be outdone, three batteries of artillery were brought up close to the Confederate front line. It proved to be the difference. Double charges of cannister tore great gaping holes in the Union line, and Southern infantry then surged forward, driving the blue-coated enemy back from the farmhouse and all the way to the northern edge of the field.

Willie expected the Yanks to re-form in the woods and try to stop the Confederate advance, but the artillery had wrecked the Union line so thoroughly that it was hopeless. What was left of a whole Yank division splintered into pieces. Some of it joined the Federal center. The rest fell back to Pittsburg Landing or retreated up the Hamburg and Savannah Road.

For a time Willie and the rest of his regiment sank to their knees, exhausted. It didn't last long. Tom Stoner ordered the third company to search the camps of the Yanks' Fourth Division for ammunition, and soon Willie and Travis were rounding up boxes of minié balls and cartridges. As they passed a Federal supply tent, Willie heard a low moan in the tall grass behind them.

Willie walked over that way and found a slight-shouldered boy of thirteen or so, propped against a large snare drum. The young man's legs hung awkwardly limp, and Willie shuddered as he saw a large red stain was spreading across the fabric of the drummer boy's tailored blue jacket.

"You come to shoot me?" the boy asked, reaching for a musket a foot or so away.

"We don't shoot prisoners," Travis said.

"My sergeant said you secesh shot anybody you got your hands on," the boy said.

"I got a sergeant tells tales himself," Willie said. "You hurtin', boy?"

"Some," the drummer boy said. "The captain said my legs are broke."

"How'd that come to be?" Travis asked.

"Captain said it was concussion," the boy said. "Cannonball landed under the wagon I was riding on. Knocked me over into a tree."

Willie looked at the solemn smile on the boy's face and turned to Travis.

"I'm stayin' here awhile, Trav," Willie said. "You go on back to the regiment with the ammunition."

"Tom won't like that, and neither will your pa," Travis said.

Willie motioned his friend over some, then whispered.

"You notice the way he's broken up, Trav?" Willie asked. "He can't last long. I'd move him to the farmhouse, but you can see. He's all stove up. It'd kill him. A dog shouldn't have to die by himself."

"You goin' soft, Willie?"

"I was born soft," Willie said. "Been gettin' harder every day since. I won't be long."

Travis turned away, and Willie walked back to the young Yank. The boy seemed to be in a lot of pain, but there was no sign of it on his face.

"What you come back for?" the drummer asked.

"I never in all my life left a boy to fend for himself," Willie said. "I come back to see what I could do to patch you up."

The boy looked at Willie with suspicion, and it touched the young Texan somehow.

Willie helped the drummer boy rest back, then opened up his jacket. The shirt underneath was soaked with blood, and Willie managed to peel that off as well. The boy shuddered once or twice, but not so much as a whimper escaped his lips.

"Musket ball?" Willie asked, tearing strips of cloth from an officer's silk shirt to bandage the wound.

"Fragment from a cannonball," the boy said.

Willie began bandaging and binding the wound, pulling it tight. But even as he did it, he knew there was no hope of stopping the bleeding. The flesh was torn to pieces, and he doubted a surgeon would've been able to save the boy.

"I figure it's pretty bad," the boy said. "They would've taken me along otherwise."

"Not too kind to drag a boy with broken legs across this country," Willie said. "Now let's have a look at the legs."

He took his bowie knife out and slit the sides of the boy's trousers open. What he saw staggered him. Both legs were shattered below the knees.

Maybe it's a blessing he's goin' to die, Willie thought to himself. Not much of a life bein' a cripple at thirteen.

"You got a Bible?" the boy asked. "My ma had a verse she used to find comfort in."

"Got one in my war chest. I might be able to scare one up in the camp up there." Willie smiled at the drummer. "I'll be right back."

It was only fifty feet or so to the supply tent, and Willie grabbed two blankets from the stack and carried them back to the dying drummer.

"Thought you might be a little cold," Willie said, draping the blankets around the young Yank's chest and legs.

"It seems so cold," the boy said, shivering.

Willie frowned. The afternoon sun was still high in the sky, and Willie's forehead was filled with sweat. The chill that worked itself through the boy was the beginning of the dying.

Willie sat with the boy in silence for a time. It was easy to see the youngster's eyes were growing glassy. There was a slurring of his speech, and Willie helped him lay down.

"Funny," the boy said. "Know why I joined up?"

"Figure you meant to free the slaves," Willie said. "That's what the rest of the Yanks I met say."

"Not me," the boy said. "Just wanted to see the other side of the Ohio," he added. "I come of a family with six girls and three boys. Me, I'm the middle one. Nobody ever paid me any mind. I guess they won't even miss me."

"Not likely," Willie said. "I'd say you were the type to be missed, missed hard."

"You don't even know me," the drummer said.

"Don't want to," Willie said. "I done enough bein' sad for men killed this day."

"My name's Micah," the boy said. "Micah Harrell, from LaSalle, Illinois."

"You want me to do somethin' for you, Micah?" Willie asked.

"Tell my ma how I died," the boy said. "Tell her how I stood my ground, died fighting for my regiment's honor."

"How'm I goin' to do that?" Willie asked.

"Do it, please," the boy said, clutching Willie's wrist.

"They may kill me an hour from now," Willie said. "I won't have myself carryin' an unkept promise to the grave with me."

"Send word then," the boy said, his voice fading. "Find somebody from the Ninth Illinois. Get them to mark my grave."

"I'll write it all down for you," Willie said, taking a piece of paper from the pocket of his tunic and using one of the dispatch pencils left from his courier duty.

As Willie wrote down the boy's name and regiment, he added something more.

"Fallen this day in the Wicker Field. Killed by a cannonball of the enemy. His death witnessed by a comrade wearing Confederate gray."

As he finished, the boy folded his hands and looked up at the sky. Willie could tell the youngster was praying, and a prayer surfaced in the young Texan's heart as well. When the moment of prayer had passed, Willie pinned his note to the boy's collar.

Willie watched as the boy wrapped an arm around the

drum. Then the simple, childlike face grew still, and the eyes stared out in eternal silence.

"I wish I had a Bible," Willie said softly, closing the boy's eyelids. "I'll tell your ma if I have a chance."

Willie covered the boy's face with a blanket and stood up. He turned away from the fallen boy and took up his rifle. Soon he was walking back to the line, heading for the sound of the guns up ahead.

13

Willie rejoined his regiment in the woods just past the Wicker Field. The firing had died down some, and word had come that thousands of Yanks in the center were now surrounded. The action in the woods was so intense the place was being called the Hornet's Nest. But with the fading of the afternoon sunlight, resistance was dying out.

Willie heard shouts then, and a Yank officer appeared with a white shirt tied to the blade of his sword.

"I am prepared to surrender my command to an officer," the Yank called out.

"I'm Colonel Bill Delamer," Willie's father announced, stepping forward to meet the enemy officer.

"I assume my men will be treated properly, colonel," the Yank said, handing over his sword.

"Your men will receive every courtesy due men who have fought bravely," Willie's father said, returning the man's sword.

Soon the woods came alive with a stream of bedraggled Union soldiers. The prisoners were escorted to the rear, and the Second Texas was ordered to take up a new position a half mile to the north.

The regiment stumbled into line with the rest of Jackson's brigade at the north edge of what was called Cloud Field. A deep ravine was all that separated the Confederates from Grant's last line at Pittsburg Landing on the Tennessee. Federal gunboats anchored in the river were shelling the Southern army, and the opposite ridge was lit by the flashes of dozens of artillery pieces.

"There lies the rest of the Yank army," a general called out to the men. "Just one more charge will carry the day."

One more charge, Willie thought to himself. He could barely stand up, and the ravine that lay between the Union line and the exhausted Confederates was hundreds of feet wide and virtually impossible to cross.

"It's just not possible," Captain Fredericks mumbled, staring at the gorge. But when Willie's father waved the men forward, not a soul refused to follow.

If the charge had been made over flat terrain, it might have had a chance of carrying the day. As it was, the weary Southern soldiers fought their way across impossible ground swept by the massed guns of the whole Federal army. Men fell in droves, and Willie could hear the whine of musket balls splitting the air all around him.

The regiment had moved to the brink of the ravine when the entire front line of the Southern advance was cut down by rifle fire. Bullets kicked up spirals of dust, and more than one hole appeared in the proud blue flag Willie was waving. The line staggered, then began to falter. As the colonel rode among the men, urging them onward with the flashing saber, he was struck twice in the chest by minié balls. A moment later the man slumped forward in the saddle and dropped the reins of the tall white horse.

"Papa?" Willie screamed, his eyes wide with shock.

"Fall back," the officers called out. "Withdraw in good order."

Willie stood there, stunned. Then he passed on the battle flag to another soldier and ran to his father. Grabbing the reins, Willie pulled himself onto the stallion's back. He wrapped an arm around the limp body of his father and allowed the colonel's head to fall against his youthful chest. Then the young corporal whipped the horse toward the safety of the Confederate line.

The entire line stumbled back to the top of the ridge. If the advance had been as rapid as the retreat, the attack might have reached the Federal line. Once back, the officers got the men down as the cannon fire adjusted to pepper the Confederate positions again.

Willie paid no attention to the bullets or the shells landing all around him. He hurried the poor horse through the soldiers, shielding his father's body with his own. When he was among the reserves, Willie dismounted and cradled the colonel's heavy body as a staff officer helped free the man's boots from the stirrups.

"Papa," Willie said as the men laid his father out on the ground.

"Willie, I'm all right," the colonel said. "Get on back to the regiment, son."

Willie turned as Major Denard appeared. The major put a hand on the young man's shoulder and drew him aside.

"You stay with the colonel, Willie," the man whispered. "Help them get him back to the Yank camps."

"Yes, sir," Willie said, looking at the worried stares on the faces of Tom Stoner and Travis Cobb.

Travis offered Willie the rifle liberated from the Yank camps earlier that day, but Willie shook his head. Then some men arrived with a stretcher, and Willie followed them away from the line.

A hospital of sorts had been set up in the camp of a Kentucky regiment on the edge of Cloud Field. It was there that the party of Texans bore the body of their wounded commander. As the others set out in search of a surgeon, Willie knelt beside his father, opening the man's shirt and binding the wounds as best he could.

Willie shook as he fought to stem the bleeding. A minié ball fired even at long range made a big hole in a man. Two such holes were in his father, one in the left side of his chest and a second slightly lower in the rib cage.

"Is it bad, son?" the colonel asked, his eyes fighting to clear themselves.

"Not so much worse than I seen before," Willie said.

"Willie, lying won't make it better. Tell me."

"Papa, two balls are in there. I'm not sure where. Looks to me like the bleedin's bad, though."

"Did we take the Yank line, Willie?" his father asked.

"No," Willie said, choking. "It was all for nothin'."

"For nothing?" the man asked feebly. "No, son, it was for something. Maybe we didn't carry the day like we intended, but we proved something."

"Proved something?" Willie asked, trembling.

"Sure, son," the man said, his lips quivering as he searched for the right words. "We showed we could endure, showed the Yanks we'd fight for what's ours. We proved we were strong."

Willie frowned. What good did it do anyone to be strong? Most of the strong ones were very dead. Maybe it was better to be weak and get back home.

Two men walked through the opening of the tent then, and Willie stood up to greet them. One was General Jackson. The other was dressed in a civilian coat.

"Corporal, you can return to your regiment now," the general said, returning Willie's crisp salute. "We'll take care of your colonel."

"Sir, I'd like to stay," Willie said. "He's my father."

The two men exchanged glances, then looked at Willie's father.

"There's cutting to be done on that man," the civilian said. "I'm no army surgeon. It's bad enough to be doing it in the middle of a battlefield. I won't have infection standing right at my elbow. Out!"

Willie didn't budge, but his father's hand reached out and touched his arm.

"Son, this is no place for company," the colonel said.

"Papa, I . . ."

"The doctor will send for you when he's done," Willie's father said. "Right, doctor?"

"It's a promise," the doctor said.

The general led Willie out of the tent, and two staff orderlies appeared with boiling water and a medical kit.

"That man's the best there is in the army," the general said. "You put your trust in him."

"Yes, sir," Willie said to the general as he left.

Willie sat down on the side of a hill and stared at the tent. He shook from head to toe, and there was no casting aside the concern that filled his insides. There'd been a kind of gnawing pain as Lieutenant Bales and others from the regiment had gone down, each in turn. And his insides had shook when news had come of General Johnston's death.

It was a different feel that came now. A great hollowness possessed him. There were no tomorrows, no more thoughts of home. If the war had been changed with the death of others, the entire world had been transformed by the two lead balls that had pierced the chest of Bill Delamer.

It was hard to lose a friend, to learn of the death of a commanding general. It tore at a man's heart to watch a boy die. But a father!

If a man like Bill Delamer, a man who'd fought the Mexicans and the Comanches, who'd carved a great ranch out of the wilderness, could be . . .

Willie didn't even want to think about it. Courage and honor were supposed to stand for something, after all. But this new kind of war was different from anything Willie had heard about. It wasn't like the newspapers said. It was killing, pure and simple, no different from shooting rabbits in the thickets behind the barn back home.

"Thought you'd be up here, Willie," Travis Cobb said to him. "The regiment's bein' pulled off the line now. Guess everybody's goin' to have a fine night's sleep."

"Sure," Willie said.

"How's your pa?"

"I don't know," Willie said. "The surgeon's in there with him now. He's got two minié balls in his chest, Trav. I never seen a man so shot up that lived. He's strong, though, and I guess maybe he's got a chance."

"'Course he does, Willie," Travis said.

But the look in their eyes betrayed the truth. Neither one of the young men expected their colonel to last the night.

As nightfall settled in, the Confederate regiments filed back into the thin line of Federal camps. All around men were looting blankets and guns and personal effects. One Alabama sergeant found a fine old guitar, and the man began playing a soft melody with a homesick tone to it.

" 'Carolina Kate,' they call it," Tom Stoner said. "All 'bout leavin' home behind."

"Here," Travis said, handing Willie a cup of steaming coffee.

"Thanks," Willie said, sipping the coffee as Travis related the latest rumors.

It grew darker, and the clouds came back. Willie stared at the dismal sky and felt himself grow empty inside. Except for the singing of the Alabama boys and the loud boom of the naval guns firing from the gunboats, the camp had grown quiet. Tom Stoner had located several boxes of cartridges, and they were doled out to the men. Willie had found some ammunition for the long rifled musket earlier, but Travis stuffed his friend's pockets with shot and cartridges.

It was close to eight o'clock when the surgeon finally left the tent where Willie's father had been taken. The man had worked over an hour on the colonel, but it was a grim look that filled the doctor's face.

Willie ran over to the tent and looked the doctor in the eye.

"How is he?" Willie asked.

"If he'd been in a hospital, if I'd gotten to it quicker, I don't know. One of the balls was deflected by a rib. It did real damage. He's a strong man to have lasted this long."

"He's still alive then?" Willie asked.

"Fading, I think," the doctor said. "I did my best for him. Now he's asking for you."

Willie passed the man and entered the darkened tent alone. A young orderly was sitting with his father, but when Willie appeared, the orderly left.

"Willie?" the colonel asked.

"I'm here, Papa," Willie said, taking his father's worn hand in his own and sitting beside the bed.

"We've come a long way from the Brazos, haven't we?" the man asked in his broken whisper of a voice.

"Some miles," Willie said, biting his lip in an effort to keep his composure.

"Jamie will likely be swimming in the river tomorrow," Willie's father said. "Just like you and Sam. Maybe he'll help with the branding this year. Henry will need some."

"Jamie's a good enough rider," Willie said. "Hasn't got the hands for ropin', but he's got the heart of a Brazos man."

"He's a little on the small side," the man said. "He'll need someone to help him grow."

"If Sam hasn't left yet . . ."

"Sam couldn't even grow himself," the colonel said, a shade of red filling his face. "You should be there to help him."

"No, you should," Willie said, his lips quivering.

"Well, I suppose when it comes down to it, a man does his own growing," Willie heard his father say with a sigh.

"That's true enough," Willie said.

"You know what I miss most?" the colonel asked.

"No, what's that, Papa?"

"Your mother's beef stew," the man said. "The way she puts in all the sage and spice."

"I miss her, too," Willie said.

"And I miss the stars at night," the man said. "I would have given my right arm for some of this rain a year or so back, but now I'd just like to feel the Texas sun on my face again."

"I know," Willie said. "It's so cold when the stars are all gone."

"They'll come back, son," his father told him. "They always do."

"Except when you're dead," Willie said softly.

"Well, I always took it to be that way, Willie. When your time comes, it comes. And I think maybe a Brazos man gets a fine life up in heaven, maybe a room with a view. There ought to be some reward for putting up with such hard cussed country here below."

"I guess so," Willie said.

"I never thought of dying much, son, and I think that's the way to live. But now I feel myself slipping away, and I guess it's just time to trust in the Lord and leave it at that."

"Papa, the doctor got the bullets," Willie said. "You're strong. Fight it!"

"Willie, I'm an old soldier. I've seen more men die than you've seen live. I know what's coming. I only wish I had more time to help you along. . . . I've never been prouder than when General Jackson's aide pointed to you and said, 'Look at that young corporal. He's what Southern soldiers are all about, hard and determined.' I imagine the sun wasn't shining any brighter than I was just then."

"I've always tried to live up to my name, sir," Willie said.

"It's a proud one, and nobody ever wore it better, his father said. Willie, I bought you a watch in Houston. It was really for your birthday, but we got taken with so many things. I never got it to you. I'd have you take it now. Travis has a likeness of his sister for you to put in it."

"Of Ellen?"

"Yes, of Ellen," the man said, a faint smile appearing on his lips. "I'm not so old as I might seem. It wasn't that many years ago that I was chasing your mama through the fields, acting like the biggest fool in Texas."

Willie took the watch and a small chain from his father. He put them carefully in his pocket, then turned his attention back to the bed.

"Remember the stories the Indians told you about the ancient ones who lived on the cliffs. Remember what I've told you of my own people, of the old Frenchman who came to America to be free. And son, build the ranch."

"I will, Papa," Willie said.

"And take care of your younger brother. Be mindful of your mama."

"Yes, Papa," Willie said, fighting to hold back the tears that were creeping into his eyes.

"You're a man now, Willie. Take my saber and be Bill Delamer."

Willie trembled as his father tried to rise. The man was too weak, though. He grasped the sword in his left hand and dragged it from its perch on a small table over to the bed. Willie took it from his father and watched the shiny scabbard flash in the dim light of the single candle burning behind them.

"Son?" the man said, his grasp growing weaker.

"Yes, Papa," Willie said coming closer.

His father then managed to put both his arms around the shoulders of his son and give him a faint embrace. Then there was a strangeness to the air, and the hands lost their grip.

Willie stared into the lifeless eyes of his father. Gently

the young man closed the eyelids, then plunged his face into the man's chest. No comfort was found there, though, and Willie pulled back, touching the saber and mumbling out a brief prayer he'd learned as a boy.

"Take him to your heart, Lord," Willie said softly. "He was a good man."

Then Willie stumbled out of the tent into the darkness, utterly lost and empty. Behind him he left the man he'd known as father, cold and dead on the side of a nameless hillside a few hundred yards from the Tennessee River.

14

Willie walked through the camp alone. The night was filled with a terrible chill, and there was a smell of rain in the air. The boom of cannons from the gunboats had come to be as ordinary as the charred stalks of corn in the fields around the camp. Only rarely was any damage done.

There was little singing in the camp now. Most of the soldiers had collapsed either inside the captured tents or under the nearby oak and pine trees. Between the lines of tents and the road was a field of the dead and the dying. Blankets liberated from the Union camps were wrapped around soldiers who would be dead by morning. The sounds of their moaning brought shivers down Willie's spine.

Walking past those suffering men, some with arms and legs cut off, others with their insides all shot to pieces, Willie was thankful his father hadn't lingered. There must have been pain, but not so bad as Willie had seen before.

Still, he hoped when his own time came that it would be quick and painless.

Willie walked for a long time, walked until his legs would hardly keep him up. Great crashes of thunder could be heard in the distance, and after a time, the rains came.

Willie had cursed the rains which had come to Corinth, which had plagued the long march from Houston. Now he was thankful they had returned. The water seemed to wash away the dust that had been stirred by the marching feet of the soldiers. Most of all, the drops of rain gathering on his forehead and trickling down his cheeks hid the warm tears which flowed like a deluge from his eyes.

Willie was surprised to find himself crying a second time in a single day. It wasn't because it was unusual for a person to cry when his father died, especially a father loved as much as Bill Delamer was by Willie. But the hardness the colonel had spoken of was a thing Willie had always had. And hard men rarely cried.

Willie thought back to what the others had told him. The general had warned him about the battle. His father had said more than once that war was no ride through the river on a Sunday afternoon. But no one could paint a true picture of the terror, of the fear and the smell and the deafening roar of battle.

No one could describe how it felt to pull a bayonet from the belly of a man whose eyes had held life a minute before. No one could put into words the stench of death that came from ten thousand dead men lying in the afternoon sun of a Tennessee April.

Yes, Willie was glad of the rain. It hid the tears, it washed away the dust. And the blood. He remembered his mother had said it best when he was but a boy. Rain came to the earth to cleanse the land, to renew life when everything had turned brown.

"Mama, it will take a flood to wash away the blood and the gore and the death from the fields of Pittsburg Landing," Willie whispered.

Looking at his feet, Willie saw that the small rivers of rain that flowed along the ground ran red with the blood of the wounded and dead on the hill. Some of the men cried out in agony, begging to be moved to shelter.

Far across the great ravine the rattle of wagon wheels could be heard. Hundreds of them. Less than a mile away the Union ranks were being swollen by reinforcements. Buell had arrived. It meant the battle was lost, that all the death and devastation had been for nought. The two Yank armies were joined, and the chance for victory which had been so bright that morning had slipped through the fingers of the Southern army forever.

Willie gave it no more thought. For him questions of victory and defeat were meaningless. War had become a personal matter, a question of living or dying. He meant to keep his mind on his own little part of the war.

His thoughts were interrupted by the sound of someone's feet splashing through the mud. He turned to face the source, one hand on the pistol in his belt.

"Willie, that you?" spoke up Travis Cobb.

"Yes," Willie said, sighing.

"You'll catch cold walking around out here in this rain," Travis said. "I saved a place for you in one of the tents."

"I'm not very good company just now," Willie said. "I'd rather be out here."

"He was a good man, your pa," Travis said. "My pa fought with him in the Mexican War. He died a brave man."

"It's small comfort," Willie told his friend.

"No, I was thinkin' on it, Willie," Travis said. "A man can't pick how he comes into this life. He's born in a stable or in a mansion, but he hasn't got any say to it. He never picks his folks, or whether he lives north or south of the Ohio. But he's got a hand in how he dies. I guess maybe that's about his most important doin', you know?"

"Papa was a fool to lead that charge," Willie said.

"No, he was Bill Delamer," Travis said. "You'd've done it, Willie. You practically outran him to take the lead, waving that fool blue flag Mrs. DeLong made up for us. I don't think it's a sad thing your pa went that way, Willie. It was the kind of death people sing songs about."

"You can't talk to a song," Willie said. "I wish I was back home, Trav. I wish we were sittin' down by the river dippin' our lines into the Brazos. I wish I was holdin' Ellie's hand at some barn dance."

"Come on to the tent, Willie," Travis said, putting a hand on his friend's shoulder. "I've got somethin' for you."

The two young Texans made their way slowly back to the tent, listening to the haunting sounds of dying men blend into the chirping of the crickets and the low hum of mosquitoes.

"Did your pa give you the watch?" Travis asked, wringing out the drenched blankets they'd used to shield themselves from the rain.

"Yes," Willie said.

"Give it to me," Travis said. "I have something for you."

Willie handed over the watch and stared as Travis crept among their sleeping comrades and took a small portrait from his cartridge belt.

"Here," Travis said, handing over the watch.

As Willie slipped out of his boots and unbuckled his belt, he gazed at the miniature portrait of Ellen. It brought a fire to his heart, filled the great hollow that had been his whole being.

"I wrote her for it while we were in Houston," Travis explained. "Your pa was goin' to give it to you, but it slipped his mind, I suppose."

"It's a good likeness," Willie said. "God, how I miss her."

"I heard Tom say somethin' 'bout you maybe goin' back to bury your pa," Travis said. "You goin'?"

"Wouldn't you?" Willie asked.

"Without havin' to be asked," Travis said. "But that's not the question I asked."

"I promised," Willie said. "But I'll come back, Trav. No Delamer ever ran from a war."

"You wouldn't be runnin', Willie," Travis said. "You're only sixteen. I figure you've done your part. No man'd hold it against you if you went back and stayed."

"Papa wouldn't've gone back," Willie said.

The inside of the tent was damp, and it was hard for Willie to find a dry place to sleep. He finally wrapped himself in a pair of blankets and faded off into a world of shadows.

There should have been peace for Willie that night, but it wasn't to be so. He found himself running again across the battlefield, watching friends fall, dodging bayonets and cannon shells. Everywhere he looked, people were shooting at him. There was no place to hide. And finally he saw his father, lying still and cold beside the surgeon.

He woke up in a cold sweat, breathing heavily. Travis was asleep beside him, and the sight warmed him a little. But he never did find any real rest that night.

15

Willie stirred that next morning to the shouts of his fellow soldiers. The men in the tent struggled to their feet, got into their damp uniforms and took up their guns. Outside the tent Major Denard was waving his sword in an effort to form the two hundred or so survivors of the previous day into some semblance of a regiment. Willie fell into one line with Travis.

"The Yanks 're comin'," Tom Stoner told them, pointing to a mass of blue-shirted infantry emerging from the far ridge, battle flags flying and drums beating.

"Buell," someone whispered.

The sight of the long lines of Yank infantry, their blue uniforms clean and bright in the early morning sunlight, was staggering. Willie felt cramps take possession of his legs. Hunger gnawed at his stomach, and his arms could hardly lift the heavy rifle to his shoulder.

"We've been ordered back to the Wicker Field, boys," the

major explained. "Form a column of fours, Captain Fredericks."

The regiment waited for the two Alabama units to lead the way, then turned to follow them down the road. The marching was hard for Willie. It hurt to give up so easily the ground his father had died to win, the fields littered with Southern dead.

The regiment filed across the open field where the Yank camps stood, smelling the thousands of dead laid out behind them. Another, different smell also filled the air. Fire. Someone was setting the Yank camps ablaze.

"That's not apt to make 'em any more friendly," Travis whispered to Willie. "Some of them boys had everything they owned in them tents."

"Most of it's headin' South," Willie said, pointing out the soldiers who were carrying armfuls of blankets, frying pans, clothing and jewelry. One private had tied a big skillet to his belt, allowing it to shield his backside.

"There's one Texas boy safe from them 'Bama sharpshooters," Travis said, laughing.

When the regiment had marched close to a mile, it began forming a line behind a battery of Alabama artillery. There was a lot of confusion in the Confederate lines. No one seemed to know who was in command or what was to be done. Scattered firing appeared to be coming from the west. Apparently the Yanks were attacking all across the front.

Some staff officer arrived and ordered the brigade back into the woods a way, but before the Texans had moved three hundred yards, a hundred Yank skirmishers raced forward toward the battery on the road, and the retreat was halted.

The Yanks overran the guns, but before they could get them hitched to horses, some of Chalmers' boys hit their left, and the men of Jackson's brigade opened up a sharp fire on the right. The Federals fell back, and the cannons were retaken.

The battery was limbered up and driven down the road toward the Peach Orchard, but the infantry stood its ground. The bloated bodies of Yank and Confederate soldiers killed in the day before's fighting were scattered all over the place, and the smell was appalling. Behind them lay Bloody Pond, its waters stained scarlet with the life's blood of the fallen. Corpses floated on the surface, their eyes frozen in horrible stares. The banks were lined with men who'd crawled to the pond during the night and died there.

The Yanks advanced again, their artillery booming out behind them. The steady lines of infantry waded through the Wicker Field, broke into the woods and surged like a swarm of blue bees toward the thin Confederate line. Willie stared at a bearded private directly ahead of him. His sights rested squarely on the man's face.

"Steady, boys," Tom spoke softly. "Wait for the order."

To the left and right Willie could hear broken volleys of rifle and musket fire as the two armies engaged. But the Federal charge closed to eighty yards or so before Tom shouted to fire.

Willie fired his rifle as the others did, and the bearded private's face exploded with the impact of a musket ball. The blue line shuddered, faltered, then knelt to fire. As Willie and the others reloaded, bullets flew through the air, and more than one Texan fell wounded or killed.

A second Texas volley destroyed the first Yank line, but a second came to take its place, and a third after that. Wave after wave of fresh Federal troops assaulted the line, and cannon fire grew intense. Finally the order to withdraw came, and the weary troops began filing back in good order. It seemed Grant had no shortage of men to throw in his charges at the weakened Southern boys holding the right flank. No fewer than ten times the Yanks had moved on the gray line, each time suffering terrible losses. But each time the enemy came back.

"They've got us on the run, and they know it," Travis said. "It's just a matter of how many we can kill before they mow down our whole army."

Willie ignored the words. He knew how a cornered animal could fight, and he saw no cowards among the regiment. The men who stood beside him were in pain. They ached from the long marches, from the fierce combat, from the hunger inside their bellies. It hurt knowing the sacrifices of the day before were all wasted. A man grows desperate when he feels enough pain.

Everything was confused. Companies and regiments fought on their own. No one was getting orders anymore, and troops were just leaving the line when they shot away their ammunition. Just as it appeared the line was holding, some regiment would withdraw, leaving a hole for the Yanks to charge.

"If General Johnston was here, things'd be different," Willie said, staring at the three balls in his hand, all that was left of his ammunition.

"Never thought I'd die on some Tennessee hillside," one of the men said as he loaded his musket. "Always thought some female down on the docks would catch up with me."

"Me, I thought I'd catch it cheatin' at cards," another man said.

It struck Willie funny. He'd never even thought about dying. It wasn't a natural thing to do at sixteen. He guessed falling there among the broken branches of the peach trees would be as good a place as another. But he'd miss the river and the cliffs, his mother and Ellen.

The last of the ammunition was shot away, and the Texas line grew quiet. When the Federals launched another charge, the regiment broke and began falling back, firing pistols and using the bayonet when it was possible. But when the Yanks pulled up a hundred yards off and fired volleys of rifle fire into the gray line, it was pull back or be massacred.

Things were coming apart on the Southern right. The Yanks had put a whole division, five or six thousand men, into the field facing what was left of three Southern brigades. Without ammunition, near exhaustion from hard fighting and little rest or food, the whole front was near collapse. Then a tall general rode up on a fine black horse and called out for Major Denard.

"Sir, when the Yanks get to the crest of that hill, I want your command to mount a charge!" the general shouted.

"Sir, we've hardly got any shot left, and . . ." the major tried to explain.

"Major, get your men moving," the general commanded. "And be careful not to fire on friendly troops. The wood is thick to your left."

"Yes, sir," Major Denard said, saluting.

The major rode along the line, passing on the general's warning about friendly troops.

The men of the regiment stared at their commander, hoping the man would have the good sense to realize how impossible a charge would be. But Major Denard simply wiped the sweat from his forehead and raised his good arm to signal the advance. Then, yelling at the top of their lungs, the Texans charged.

The Yanks on the ridge ahead froze as the gray mass moved on them. They were men who'd not yet heard the terrible rebel yell, and they hesitated. Even their officers seemed surprised. As the crest of the hill neared, soldiers sprang out of the woods on the left, but Major Denard ignored them.

"Just more Southern boys joining our line," the major said confidently.

But the infantrymen in the wood wore blue uniforms, and the volley of rifle fire they uncorked shattered the Second Texas. The air was alive with minié balls, and Willie found himself running as never before. The regiment fled down the ridge, caring nothing for who won the battle or what had happened the day before. The sole thought of the men was to avoid the blistering fire of the Yanks in the woods.

"Stop, cowards!" the general cried out, waving his saber at the Texans. "Halt, you men!"

Even the officers were running, though, and the general, his face red with rage, charged into the midst of the men and began firing his pistol in the air.

"Stop, you cowards, or I'll shoot you myself!" the general shouted.

But the soldiers were past the point of caring. Willie and Travis dove into a ravine and sat there, shivering as the Yanks began firing at them again.

"Re-form!" Willie heard Major Denard yell. "Rally to the flag, boys!"

But Willie's feet were frozen. He sat there, cowering in the ravine with Travis Cobb.

"You men get out of there!" a staff officer commanded, riding along the ravine and using the flat end of his saber to move the men back to their units.

"Get going there!" the officer yelled, firing his pistol into the ground a hundred yards or so back of where Willie stood.

"Come on, boys," Tom Stoner said, walking over to them. "We've got a job to do."

The voice of duty stirred Willie at last, and he crawled out of the ravine, dragging his empty rifle along behind him.

16

The Southern line didn't manage to re-form until it reached the wooded ground just east of the Peach Orchard. The Federals were tangled in the brush and ravines which had stalled the Confederate attacks only yesterday, and it gave Willie and the others a chance to catch their breath.

"Boys, we mean to hold this ground," Major Denard said to the men, waving his sword over his head. "Texans died winning these fields. Friends and neighbors we'll not see again fell to take this place. Brothers and fathers, sons and nephews who will sing no more songs, march no more roads, bled and died here. We have paid the price with our suffering, with our blood. We will not hand it back to the enemy without a price being paid. Such would not be fitting."

The men began to stir to the words. A new determination filled their faces. Men who'd been ready to run minutes before now sharpened their bayonets and readied themselves for the task ahead.

"Rally to the colors, boys!" Tom Stoner called out again, grabbing the blue flag and waving it in the air. "Stand your ground and carry the day!"

The men began pounding the ground with the butts of their muskets, creating a loud and comforting noise. The sound made their nerves sharp, kept away the loud explosions of the Federal cannons. Suddenly they were a regiment again, and when the blue-coated Yanks charged into their midst, the thin line of Texans held their ground and stung the enemy hard.

Willie's feet began to move, and he swung his rifle low so that the sharp bayonet on the end rested low and level with the others all around it. Tom Stoner was in the lead, waving his company on. Men trampled the wounded and the dead, howled like banshees and turned the Yank advance into a stampeding retreat.

The Texans had become veterans in a day's time, and the Yanks opposite them were still green troops. The difference began to tell as the blue-shirted regiment yielded first the road, then the ground beyond. Men dropped their rifles, their sabers, everything that weighed them down. Soon the Southerners held up, allowing the enemy to race back behind the safety of a wall of cannons.

But the Yanks weren't beaten, merely repulsed. They came again and again, and the Confederate bayonets flashed until the road ran red with blood. Men in blue and men in gray fell side by side. A wall of humanity rose up along the road, holding back the charges of either side. Such a fight seemed impossible. No man could endure the heat and the death. But fight on they did, losing and gaining ground, killing and being killed. At last a deadly volley of rifle fire staggered the gray line, forcing it to yield the road and retire to its original line of defense.

Willie fought to catch his breath as he stared at the piles of corpses in the road ahead of him. Twenty or thirty more of the regiment's dwindling numbers had fallen, but the enemy had paid dearly. Near twice that number of Yanks lay there, frozen forever in the grasp of death.

"We showed 'em that time, major!" someone yelled out.

"We held our ground!" another man shouted.

Willie found no time for cheering or celebrating. The Yank guns crept closer, and it was only a matter of time before a fresh charge was mounted. He slowly began to realize that the major intended the regiment should stand and die on that very spot, hold on until ordered back. Few orders of any kind came now. General Jackson was nowhere to be found, and the closest thing to a field commander was General Hardee, the Third Corps commander who had little regard for the Second Texas after watching them fail in the charge on the distant ridge.

The Yanks finally re-formed. Willie recognized some new battle flags this time, and it was clear a fresh regiment had been brought up. He swallowed deeply and waited for the enemy. Stirring blasts of bugles split the air, and a roll of drums began.

Terrible holes were torn in the Union lines by small iron balls fired by Alabama artillery. Willie watched in horror as men lost arms and legs. Trunkless heads rolled down the hill, sickening the Southern defenders and the Northern attackers. Soon the two lines met again, and the clash of sabers and bayonets grew heated.

Willie had seen nothing like this fight, not even in the camps of the Comanches. Men fought like dogs, kicking and clawing and hitting each other with anything they could find. Men found themselves crawling along on their elbows, ducking behind fallen trees in the faint hope of escaping the madness.

In the middle of the melee stood Tom Stoner, urging his soldiers on. One after another of the Yanks went after old Tom, but the Indian fighter held his ground and killed each in turn. But two young riflemen stopped and fired their rifles at Tom Stoner. The old veteran of the Mexican War was hit twice in the belly, and he howled out in pain.

Willie remembered Tom talking about belly wounds. Perhaps that explained the madness that came over the man. As the Yanks retreated, Tom took up a saber dropped by a dead officer and set out after the Yanks. It was a one man charge. The Texan, his uniform covered with blood and the blueness of death on his lips, ran after the two Yank riflemen and cut them down. Then he started hacking others. Finally a volley cut him down.

Willie, Travis, and three others ran after him, and the rest of the Yanks fell back. When they reached Tom, the sergeant was dead.

Now command of the company passed to Willie. There was little organization left to the regiment, though. Only a hundred and fifty men remained in the line, the remainder having straggled to the rear or been killed or wounded in the fighting.

It came down to standing with friends or relatives. Willie and Travis were surrounded by others who'd ridden out from the Brazos with Bill Delamer.

The Texans surged forward to meet the Yank attack once more. It was like a horde of wolves escaped from hell. They hacked with sabers, stabbed with bowie knives, clubbed with rifles, and jabbed with bayonets. By some miracle the charge shattered the Federal line, carried through the woods and began flowing up the ridge toward a Federal battery.

Suddenly the ridge exploded with shellfire. Southerners charging and Northerners fleeing were caught together by furious volleys of minié balls and cannister. Men were swept away everywhere, and the field was covered with their limp bodies. The man ahead of Willie turned and lunged toward him with a bayonet, and Willie felt his shoulder burn with pain. A minié ball nicked the young corporal's scalp and carried away his hat.

Staring at the Yank, Willie swung his own rifle around and sank the bayonet on the end of it deep into the center of the man's blue uniform tunic. Blood oozed from the deep wound in the man's belly, and Willie watched the man's eyes die.

"Willie?" Travis called to him from behind.

Willie tried to keep his eyes clear. The rest of the regiment had begun creeping back down the ridge. He felt his fingers lose their hold on the rifle, felt his shoulder explode as the bayonet slid back out of his body. Warm red blood flowed onto his neck and dripped down his forehead.

For a moment the whole world stood still, frozen in time. Willie's eyes watered, and a fog filled his brain. He fell back, rolling along the rocky ridge until a log stopped him.

17

WILLIE'S HEAD WAS CLOUDY, but he didn't lose consciousness. His hand fumbled around, trying to draw out the pistol that rested in his belt. The ground around him shook as a cluster of cannon balls tore great holes in the field. Any second he expected to feel the sharp sting of another bayonet.

Then something warm, friendly grasped his shoulders.

"It's all right, Willie," Travis told him.

"Trav?" Willie asked feebly.

"You just tuck that pistol back in your belt and stay put," Travis said, tearing strips of cotton from a shirt to bind Willie's shoulder.

"Best get out of here," Willie said faintly.

"Be still," Travis said, tightening the binding. "I'm takin' you out of here."

Travis slung Willie's thin body over his back and began running across the field. The Yanks weren't a hundred yards behind, and the ground around them was peppered with rifle fire. But as the two young men neared the Confederate line, a squadron of cavalry appeared to shield them and break the spearhead of the Yank charge.

Travis helped Willie back to the Yank camps. There was no surgeon to field dress the wound, but some whiskey was located to clean away the dirt, and the wound was rebound.

"I'll get you on a wagon, Willie," Travis promised.

"What wagon?" Willie asked. "There's no wagon to be found around here."

"I'll find one," Travis said.

"You'd best get back to the regiment," Willie told his friend. "The provosts . . ."

"Hang the provosts!" Travis said. "I'll find a wagon if I have to liberate one from the Yanks."

Willie sat for what seemed an eternity, alone and without hope. He faded in and out of consciousness, probably due to the large bump he could feel on his head. But finally Travis returned with four or five soldiers from the Second Texas, and the men managed to carry him along in a blanket stretcher when the army began its retreat toward Corinth.

"The center and left have caved in, Willie," Travis whispered to him. "They're talkin' about marchin' all the way back to Corinth tonight."

"Then it's over," Willie mumbled. "We've lost it all, Tennessee, the army . . ."

"The army's still here," Travis said. "Every mile we move back some man we thought lost comes back to the regiment."

Willie frowned. He was thinking about his father and

General Johnston. The army's heart had been shot away. There was no other Albert Sidney Johnston to inspire the men, no Bill Delamer to lead the final charge.

Travis finally found Willie a place in an empty supply wagon. The captain driving the wagon had known Bill Delamer in Mexico, and when two dead men were taken off, he allowed Willie to take their place.

"Is it a bad wound?" the captain asked. "We're apt to be on the road for hours, and it won't be a gentle journey."

"He's strong," Travis said, "and the bleeding seems to have stopped."

So it was that the Texans slid Willie into the back of the wagon next to a young lieutenant wearing the snappy uniform of the Orleans Guards. The regiment had been hit hard, and most of the wounded in the wagon had been a part of it.

Willie stared at the lieutenant while Travis put two extra blankets taken from the Federal camps on top of his friend. Then Willie glanced back at Travis and smiled.

"If I don't make it, Trav, tell Ellie yourself," Willie said softly. "Don't write it in a letter or send a wire."

"I'll see it comes from a friend," Travis said. "Most likely you yourself. At least you get a ride back to Corinth. We'll be walkin'."

Willie tried to laugh at the pretended complaint, but laughter wasn't in him just then. As his friends left him to fall in with the regiment, Willie closed his eyes and sought the peace that sleep might bring.

The peace didn't come, though. The road along which the wagon traveled had suffered much from the rains. Deep ruts crisscrossed its entire length, and the wounded men were jolted every few minutes or so. No speed could be made, either. Long columns of troops stretched as far as the eye could see, and the pace of the vehicle was governed by the methodical plodding of thousands of weary legs.

For a time Willie stared at the face of the young lieutenant next to him. Some surgeon had amputated the man's right arm on the field, and although the bleeding had stopped, the man's eyes were hazy, and there was a feverish look about his forehead.

"Likely he's about to die," the private next to him whispered. "Too bad. He was a brave one. Was talkin' all 'bout his sweetheart while back. I thought he was goin' to start bawlin'."

"Seems a man's entitled on his deathbed," Willie said. "Lieutenant, can we do anythin' for you?" Willie asked, wiping the sweat from the officer's forehead with a discarded handkerchief.

"You sound Texas to me," the private said. "Name's Tom D'Orne. Come from Lake Charles."

"Willie Delamer," Willie said, nodding to the private.

"Carolina," the lieutenant mumbled. "Carolina."

"That a girl or a place?" Willie asked.

"Don't know," Tom said. "I think maybe a girl."

"Somebody tell the driver," Willie said. "Maybe he can do somethin'."

"No man can do anything for him," an old sergeant who'd lost both legs said from across the wagon. "He'll be seeing paradise soon."

"Lieutenant?" Willie whispered.

"Son, don't waste your time," the sergeant said. "He's got what he wanted."

"What?" Willie asked.

"Carolina, the girl," the sergeant said. "She ran off with his brother. He joined up to get killed. When the Yanks didn't do the job, he took a knife and cut himself."

Willie noticed then that the bleeding came not from the lieutenant's arm but from a great gash down his side.

"He killed himself, and with two legs, too," the sergeant said. "Don't you pity him, son. Not with us all here dying, and he with a chance to sit out his days in a manor house with darkies doing all his work for him. No, sir, don't you have pity on that man."

Willie shrank back a bit. Soon the lieutenant's eyes closed, and there was the smell of dying. Someone near the front banged three times on the side of the wagon, and the driver slowed to a stop. One of the more able of the wounded pushed the lieutenant out of the wagon, and Willie stared in horror as the man's body rolled in the mud, then was driven over by another wagon.

"They could've pulled him to the side of the road," Willie said.

"What does it matter?" Tom said. "Dead is dead."

"Wouldn't you want to be buried in a churchyard?" Willie asked. "Wouldn't you want somebody to read words of comfort over your bones."

"Willie, I never lived myself much of a churchy kind of life. I figure to rot in hell one way or t'other. Seems like some dog ought to at least get a good meal off me."

Willie felt himself grow sick, and it was all he could do to keep from vomiting.

"Never you mind, son," the legless sergeant said, sliding over to the lieutenant's place. "He's as scared of dying as the rest of us. Only too dumb to take solace in the name of the Lord."

"You gone preacher, huh, sergeant?" Tom asked. "You tell me then, if God's around, how come he let somethin' happen like what we seen today? You tell me that?"

"The fires of his wrath hath visited upon the land," the sergeant said. "The mark of Cain has been placed on the face of man so that brother will kill brother."

"Somebody shoot that preacher," a soldier said from the other side of the wagon. "Let me die in peace."

Willie drifted off about then, and his head was possessed by a beautiful dream of spring along the Brazos. He ran with Ellen through the water, felt the warmth of her hand at his side. Then a terrible cry woke him, and he watched a soldier writhing in pain.

"His dressing's broke loose," someone said. "Help him."

But no one got there, and the man screamed out a final time. Then blood oozed from his mouth, and his eyes closed.

"Dump him," the sergeant said, passing the limp body down the line until it reached Tom and Willie.

"Get the driver to pull over," Willie said.

"Never mind," Tom said, pulling the body out of the wagon. "Let the dead tend to themselves."

Willie pushed himself as far away as possible from the private then.

"I'll bet he's the next one to go, sergeant," a bearded private said, pointing to a corporal in the corner opposite Willie. "How 'bout it? Ten dollars says he's next."

"I'll take that," another man said. "I figure it's got to be that private beside him."

They went on to wager. It was the man in the corner, though, and soon another body was tossed out into the muddy road.

"God, forgive them," Willie mumbled.

"You keep your God," Tom said. "Now who bets on the kid in the back, the one from Georgia?"

Willie closed his eyes and tried to ignore it all. The wagon had passed most of the retreating troops by then, and its pace grew quicker. It wasn't but sixteen more miles to Corinth, someone said, and Willie mustered his strength to keep himself alive until he could get back there, until some kind of help could be reached.

He faded off then, sailing above the clouds to a different kind of place. His father was there. So were little Stephen and his sister Christine, who'd been stillborn. Willie sat down with them, smiling as Stephen laughed the way he had until that terrible winter of '56 had taken him with a fever.

"You were a brave man, Willie," his father said, "but I wish you'd taken me home."

Other images flew through his mind. There were old times full of laughter and adventure, days yet to be darkened by the clouds of war and death.

"He's heavy," someone said, putting his hands on Willie's shoulders.

"Come on, pass him along," Tom said.

"No!" Willie screamed, pushing them away. "No!"

The others drew back from him, and the sergeant angrily punched Tom in the face.

"You foul scum!" the sergeant screamed. "Told us he was dead!"

"He's near enough," Tom said. "Won't last the trip, I tell you. Lighter the load, the faster this wagon'll get us back to Corinth."

"You put a hand on that boy again, I'll borrow his pistol and blow your brains out," the sergeant said. "I wouldn't purchase my life at the cost of a boy like that."

"I would," Tom said. "Look at you anyway. What kind of a blacksmith has no legs? Maybe we ought to cast you both out."

"You just try," Willie said, taking the pistol out of his belt and cocking it. "You ready to die, Tom? Just where are you shot, anyway?"

The other men mustered their anger at the Louisiana private, and Willie read fear in Tom's eyes. Someone grabbed the man's bloody shirt and tore it open. There wasn't even a hint of a wound.

The sergeant took the pistol from Willie, but before it could be fired, Tom jumped out of the wagon and rolled in the dust of the road. Then he raced for the trees, reaching cover before the sergeant could fire.

"Pig!" a private from his regiment said, spitting out the

back of the wagon. "His ma and mine were friends, too. There's one man who can't go home."

Willie thought over the words. They were terrible. What did a man do who couldn't go home?

The thought flooded his mind, and his hand weakly took the pistol back from the sergeant and uncocked the hammer. With the gun securely back in his belt, Willie collapsed again, this time falling into a deep slumber which even the rough road and the jolts of the wagon were unable to disturb.

18

Willie wasn't aware of what happened after that. When his head finally cleared enough for him to open his eyes, a soft face dressed in white smiled down at him in the candlelight of a large room.

"Mama," Willie mumbled, reaching for the shadowy hand of the figure beside him.

"Rest easy, son," a delicate voice said with a smooth southern accent. "You'll be just fine now."

"Mama?" Willie said a second time, fighting to clear his head.

"I'm not your mother, son, but you're welcome to take my hand as if I was," the voice said.

Willie took the woman's hand and squeezed it.

"Who are you?" Willie asked. "Where am I?"

"You are in my home in Corinth, young man," the woman said. "I am Mrs. Amanda Johnson. You brave young men have thrashed the Yanks soundly up by Shiloh Church."

"We won?" Willie asked.

"Near drove the blue-coated snakes right into the Tennessee River," Mrs. Johnson told him. "We rang the bells here for three straight hours."

"What happened? The last I remember we were pulling back here. Did the army counterattack? Did Van Dorn arrive?"

"No, son," Mrs. Johnson said. "We withdrew here as planned after whipping those Yankees."

Willie looked into the woman's eyes and quieted his own thoughts. If it was a victory, it certainly was a hollow one.

"A young man named Cobb came to see you yesterday," Mrs. Johnson told Willie. "He will be back sometime this afternoon."

Willie felt a faint smile come to his lips. He released the woman's hand and reached for the watch. His clothes were gone, though, and the timepiece with them. As Willie searched frantically, Mrs. Johnson touched his forehead in a way that calmed him.

"You clothes were taken to be washed," she told him. "I offered one of my son John's nightshirts for you. You must see that the shoulder is so much more likely to mend where there's no dirt around."

"Yes, ma'am," Willie said. "Thank your son for me."

"It's beyond that," Mrs. Johnson said, her face turning white and sour, but not giving way to emotion. "He was killed the first day."

"I'm sorry," Willie said. "I lost my father toward nightfall that day."

"It was a heavy price to pay for freedom," Mrs. Johnson said. "My husband, Henry, fell in the first charge, and my youngest, Philip, was killed in the twilight of battle. I lost a nephew as well with Colonel Forrest's cavalry. It was a dark day for our family."

"I'm sorry for you, ma'am," Willie said.

"They said your name is William," she said.

"It was my grandfather's name," Willie said. "My father called himself Bill, and I use Willie."

"You remind me of Philip," she said, smoothing out his tangled hair. "He was blond, too, though not so dark in color. He turned sixteen this year, and there was no keeping him out of the army."

"I'm sixteen myself," Willie told her.

"You ought to be away to school then," Mrs. Johnson said. "Boys ought to be walking the promenade with a debutante on each arm, sipping lemonade and listening to Mozart and Schubert."

"Well, ma'am, I suppose sometimes sixteen is an age to be a man," Willie said. "If a cause is worthy, then it's a man's right to give away his life in its behalf."

"That's true enough," Mrs. Johnson said. "My Henry surely felt that way. And there are some in the army as young as fourteen. Still, it's hard on a woman to nurse a child, rock him on her knee and dry his tears, only to have him killed by some Yank on a godforsaken hill you've never even seen."

"I guess that's true, ma'am."

"I must be along now to sit with the other men. My

daughter Emily will be coming by to see you later. I hope you will allow her to share your company. She misses her brothers, and there are no respectable young men about Corinth in these times."

"That'd be fine, ma'am," Willie told the woman as she left.

Willie slipped off into a light sleep for a time. It was a gentle, peaceful kind of world that came to him. His eyes opened when something touched his hand.

"Trav?" Willie mumbled, staring up at the face of his old friend.

"You look better today," Travis said. "Thought there for a while you might not make it."

"They grow 'em tough out our way."

"The doctor spent some time hackin' away at that shoulder of yours."

"I knew I was feelin' lighter," Willie said.

"Well, if you got that Texas humor of yours back, Willie Delamer, I expect you'll be racin' horses 'fore too much longer."

"Might be a while yet before that," Willie said. "I feel like my shoulder's been nailed to this bed."

"Does it hurt much?" Travis asked, a frown spreading across his face.

"I've felt worse," Willie said. "That time I got pitched into that den of rattlers down by Bluff Creek, for one."

"Just about had to bury you that day," Travis said.

They spoke awhile about times spent as children in the land far to the west. There was talk of Ellen and mothers and even of hunting deer. But finally a more serious moment came, a moment Willie had not longed for.

"I brought you the sword, Willie," Travis said, lifting the weapon and setting it close to his side so that Willie could touch it with his good right hand.

"Where's Papa?" Willie asked, a tremble working through him.

"In the basement of an ice house," Travis said. "I got a woman to wash him, and we put him in a new uniform. He looks just grand, Willie, really he does."

"He asked me to take him home," Willie said softly.

"Well, it's for sure you'll do a fine job of that with a shoulder you can't even get out of bed."

"I promised to get him back, Trav. I mean to get it done. Truth is, I couldn't go back anyway. I'm a soldier now."

"You aim to stick it out, huh? Yanks'll take Memphis 'fore long. That means fallin' back hereabouts, some say all the way to Jackson. Or headin' up to Virginia. Some of the regiments say they're headin' up there first chance."

"Trav, you suppose you might . . ."

"I'm no less a soldier than you are, Willie Delamer," Travis said. "But I guess I know what's in your heart. You know old Dan Benton?"

"Sure," Willie said, his eyes showing confusion.

"Dan lost his left arm," Travis said. "Just below the elbow. It's healin' up fine, but he plans to go home. I did some talkin' to a man down by the railway. There's a train goin' south to Jackson, then west to Monroe, Louisiana. That's halfway, at least, and there's roads most of the way from there. It's open country from Fort Worth, but a man like old Dan can handle it."

"You did some figurin' on this, didn't you?" Willie asked. "I thank you for that, Trav."

"If things were t'other way around, Willie, you'd do it for me. We both know that. You want to see him 'fore the train pulls out this evenin'? There's not another train for five days."

"No, I said my good-byes," Willie said. "You best send him along. I'd have you write a letter to go with him, though."

"You best get Mrs. Johnson to do that for you, Willie," Travis said. "I never did much writin'. Get my letters mixed up sometimes."

"I'll do that," Willie said.

"Ellen'd take it kind if you sent her word as well," Travis said. "I know her heart's savin' a place for you, and I see you got the watch out."

"Yes," Willie said, opening it up again to gaze at Ellen's face.

They shared most of the afternoon. Then Travis left to report in at regimental headquarters, and Willie turned to the letter writing.

It was Mrs. Johnson's daughter, Emily, who did the writing, and Willie was pleased Travis had suggested it. Looking at Emily's blond hair brought back the feelings of longing and affection that had become hidden away deep in his heart. When both letters were finished, Willie managed to sign his name. Emily then rushed the letters to the station so that Dan Benton could carry them home with Willie's father.

A peace settled over Willie that night. For the first time since leaving the Brazos the young man knew a sense of belonging and inner tranquility.

19

WILLIE FELT HIMSELF GETTING BETTER during the following week. His legs were solid as ever, and the headaches which had bothered him in the days following the battle had grown less and less common. He breathed easier, though hard laughing still brought a reaction from the tender muscles in his shoulder.

Corinth, too, was beginning to recover from the shock of combat. Although the city had not yet been shelled or raided, scarcely a household had not felt to some extent the calamity of the battle, dubbed Shiloh after the small Methodist meetinghouse. Among the dead in the Mississippi regiments were sons and husbands, fathers and cousins. Many of the finer houses had, like Mrs. Johnson's, been converted into makeshift hospitals.

Recovery in the army was not quite so apparent. The camps were still filled with wounded, many of them seriously hurt. The battle had taken its toll of officers, from

General Johnston on down. New colonels and lieutenants were arriving daily from different state capitals, some stepping off trains only to find their regiments had moved on the day before.

Some units moved toward Virginia to fight with the army in defense of Richmond. Others were assigned to garrison forts or shore batteries on the Mississippi. Most stood in their camps, though, waiting for the Union army now estimated to number a hundred thousand men to fall upon the city of Corinth itself.

The people Willie saw were grim. A Confederate stronghold on the Mississippi had fallen, and Federal gunboats were cruising the river as far south as Memphis. There was talk of Yank armies attacking the forts guarding New Orleans. The city of Corinth itself was safe only as long as the Yanks sat around their camps on the Tennessee and sang their songs.

The Yanks wouldn't stay forever, though. By late spring or early summer they were bound to take the city, sealing the fate of Memphis and severing the rail link to the western states. All of eastern Tennessee would be in Federal hands. It wouldn't be long before the very heart of the Confederacy was under attack. With no Sidney Johnston to inspire a bold attack, with the best of her men lying in the cold earth, victory was a forlorn hope.

What was left would be a war of defiance, a slow gradual yielding of ground, with Southern armies exacting a price in blood as the cost of subjugation. Time and pride would be bought at the price of humanity.

"You could take your wound and go home, Willie," Emily whispered to him on the street that day. "No one would think the less of you. Travis says you fought with courage, and there's your family and Ellen to consider."

"I'll go home," Willie said sadly. "I'll return when the generals all lay down their swords, when the president in Richmond or wherever says to us the fight is won. Or lost."

"You'll most likely be killed," she said, shaking her head. "I will never understand the stubbornness of men."

"You do understand," Willie said. "It's what brings your mother to turn her house into a hospital, what makes Mrs. Morris spin homespun gray cloth for uniforms. Southern women are no less stubborn, no quicker to yield."

She'd smiled at that.

A month later, wearing the fresh insignia of a lieutenant, Willie watched the Second Texas pull out of Corinth as the Yanks under Grant moved at last against the city.

With him stood his old friend, Travis Cobb, now a corporal, and two hundred Texas cavalrymen who'd served with Van Dorn in Arkansas, and were now bound for Richmond with orders to join General Hood's brigade.

Willie couldn't help frowning as the men marched south, disheartened and defeated. Less than four hundred remained, and many of those were sick or wounded. A new colonel had arrived from Austin, together with a cluster of lieutenants fresh from the academies of Houston and New Orleans.

"Virginia's a long way off," Travis whispered to him then.

"I've heard that," Willie said.

"We were a fine regiment when we marched into this town," Travis said, smiling as he remembered.

"Yes, we were like wildcats," Willie said.

But in his heart he'd learned the lesson his father had tried to put into words. He'd come to know the face of battle, to feel the sharp-edged sword of war. And he'd learned to know the smell of death and see the darkness that can possess the hearts of men.

He didn't know then what would follow. His eyes could not gaze into the future and watch the remnant of the proud regiment lay down its arms fourteen months later at Vicksburg, while he was half a continent away charging the Little Round Top near a town called Gettysburg.

If he'd known the blood that would flow those next three Aprils, if any of them had known, perhaps someone might have put a stop to it. But those men who can see at all never know but the present. And so they charge blindly into the future.

On rainy nights in April, there are those who hear the voices of ghosts singing battle hymns or murmuring prayers. But there are no more stirring drum rolls or bayonet charges for the men who once fought at Pittsburg Landing. The last of the soldiers lay quiet in the earth, and it is only for those who would remember the past to speak of what happened there, where the Tennessee once surged and young men spent their lives for something called glory or honor.